The Drakon King

The Drakon King

Book one of
The War of Five Kings

Carlton N. Brock III

Book and cover design by Ally Ruiz Talcott
ISBN 979-8-9939781-0-9

Prologue

In the beginning, Earth was home to only the Humans, the Elves, and the Dwarves. Those early times saw the three races interact sparingly and rarely if ever speak. That was until the discovery of magic.

As with the inhabitants of all the great planets, Earthlings found themselves able to use and manipulate magic. Unlike nearly every other planet, the citizens of Earth found themselves able to use magic as diverse as they were. Wars sprung about the map like flowers in a field. Technology advanced in a way that it possibly wouldn't have in Earths of other timelines.

Soon the magic gave birth to Orcs. Then their counterparts, the Orc-Men and the Orc-Elves. Vampires, Werewolves, and other horrific manifestations followed suit. All were the result of the Earthling's pursuit of understanding and their greater pursuit of war.

Earth is the so called "Golden Egg" of planets in the universe. It is able to sustain life. It has an atmosphere. It has liquid water. These are rare traits in naturally occurring planets. That is not what makes Earth special, there are thousands of planets with these traits amongst millions in the known universe. What makes Earth special amongst special planets is it's central location amongst the magical realms.

Where species of most planets can only access one or possibly two types of magic, the Mages of Earth can use several types without consequence. Once Earthlings discovered their strategic advantage, the great wars of Earth seemingly came to an end, replaced with an interplanetary conquest.

This led to the consolidation of all governments under the Kingdom of the Flock under the first king, The Drake King. Generations later, most of the descendants of the colonists and knights have never seen their Homeworld, the Earth. To maintain order, the Drake King established the Knights of the Flock to act as both peace keepers and an offensive force.

Children that were selected to become Squires were given this history lesson every year until they were given the full rank of Squire in the Knights of the Flock. Upon becoming a Squire, they would go through the most sacred of rituals. In exchange for joining the ranks of the Knights of the Flock, their names and records would be erased forever.

While trillions of lives in the known universe accept this reality in the Kingdom of the Flock as their rulers and protectors, just as many believed that there were others more suitable to rule. Many attempted to overthrow the Drake King and many fell for they were not chosen by fate to rule.

In time, the Knights of the Flock became just as focused on maintaining and even expanding their kingdom as they were defending their people. War broke out amongst the citizens of the ever-expanding kingdom. Eventually the great and powerful Drake King fell. In his stead several Kings rose and fell until the peaceful ruler, The Drakon King ascended to power.

The Drakon King established a Peace that henceforth been unseen in the tumultuous space largely by limiting magic to something people could only access by chance rather than by decision. But peace cannot last forever. Our story takes at the end of this peace as the War of Five Kings begins…

Act 1: The Squires

Chapter 1

The sky was a lie. It was unmoving. The clouds coming into view occasionally blinked with a data refresh. Sometimes the sky would make a sudden shift into night mode. Only for a split second everything would go completely black, like a lightbulb flicker. Newer ships, like The Resolution, Raven's home. didn't have these problems. The sky was still a lie, but there weren't as many issues.

Every ship built after the launch had synthetic gardens. They all had fresh fruits and vegetables. They all had beautiful grass that was specifically modified to never require so much as a trim. They all had mechanical bees pollinating the vegetation. The gardens in the ships were marvels of pre-launch technology. They were beautiful.

But the sky was still a lie.

Raven had never seen what the real Earth sky looked like. He had only ever seen pictures that his grandfather brought with him on launch day. Not to say that he had never seen a sky, he wasn't sure his mother had even seen an Earth sky. Raven had seen the azure sky of Neptune, the orange sky of Mars, and skies of hundreds of other worlds. He had been so close to the Homeworld, but never saw it.

"Mom," Raven would start every so often as a child, "how come the sky is so blue."

"Because that's what it looks like on Homeworld." She would say.

"Is Homeworld the only place with a blue sky?" He would always reply.

"Certainly not. We just haven't been to one this beautiful shade of blue yet." She told him at least a thousand times.

He observed the synthesized space around him. The mud squished beneath his boots. Bugs would occasionally land on his overcoat. When he was out on missions, Raven preferred wearing bandanas over his mouth like an old west cowboy in addition to his black and purple light armor. He looked around the empty room as he pulled the bandanna over his mouth and started to leave. It felt like he was waking from dream.

A short while later, Raven returned to his room to prepare for launch. He packed his bag with four rations worth of freeze-dried fruits and vegetables. He didn't need this much, he would be back within a Homeworld Lunar Cycle, but he wouldn't risk it. Raven had known from many failed missions before that he knew how quickly it could go wrong.

Next, he packed his beam sword and katana. Raven was always sure to bring both in case the batteries in his sword ran out. With his bag packed, Raven was ready to take on the world.

Chapter 2

Crow looked down at his training partner, a puppet. Not a full-sized golem, just a puppet that he made out of spare parts stuffed into a body made from a burlap sack. He made puppets from anything he could find, golem parts, ship parts, skeletons, machines, even children's toys. Tinkering them into existence with magic was his favorite hobby. Practicing martial arts with them was proof of his personal belief that if he was going to command magical creatures he needed to be able to do any and every thing that he ordered them to do.

Inverted Berimbolo to leg lock? Crow could do it, so could his puppets, so could his golems. Muay Thai knee to chest? Crow could do it. He wasn't a proficient spell caster or swordsman, but one in ten thousand people were able to control golems and even fewer of them could summon them from anywhere.

Crow stared down at his hands as they gripped the finger of the puppet. If he were a citizen of Homeworld, his hands would be registered as weapons of mass destruction. At least, that was the persistent rumor. Spell casting didn't work like that. A mage needed only know what they intended to do and have enough power to perform it. Some Mages used hands, some used books, some used wands, some used only the words they spoke. It was all about how they channeled their energy which was as individual as ones fashion sense.

Mages needed to have an affinity toward the type of magic they were using. Some people spent years training to develop their magical energy. Mostly to no avail. It wasn't a muscle. Exercises didn't build magical energy. Training could only fine tune how to use the magic that an individual had access to. So called "Magic schools" were just a farce. The oft mentioned "Magic words" were a lie as well. No word was more magical than any other. Crow believed that magical power could only be increased by requirement. Nothing more, nothing less. If all someone ever used magic for was creating a light, that would be their maximum output.

Magic knew if it was truly required. It always knew. This was the reason mages and summoners became fewer and farther in between as technology developed. Magic decided that less people required it. Others didn't share this belief. Crow had at times taken advice and done training if only to fine tune his own natural gifts. But he still didn't believe he needed it. Eventually, he believed, he would develop on his own. Crow believed he was special.

He positioned his weight so he was resting on top of the puppet's head while facing the puppets feet. The puppet's arm was bent at a ninety degree angle while he held its wrists in position for a Kimura lock. Crow moved his hand slightly forward and clutched the puppet's index finger with his left hand. He waved his right hand to make a door materialize beneath the puppet. It was a plain wooden door with the word "Crow" etched into it, functionality over form.

He broke the puppet's finger. It let out an almost- human sounding scream before disappearing into the magical door. It was a cruel move to say the least, but he was certain that the puppet only felt pain because Crow wanted it to. Cruelty was not something Crow considered when preparing for a mission. If he needed to be cruel to save lives, it was a necessary choice. He walked to his locker and grabbed his mask which wrapped around the bottom half of his face. It bore resemblance to a wendigo skull though the canine teeth were much thicker.

Chapter 3

Puffin, the lieutenant under Knight Commander Hummingbird, was responsible for all squires as they prepared to move into full life as knights. He assigned missions. He decided when tests would be assigned. In a way, Puffin hated his job as much as he loved it. He finalized the code names, each Knight named after a bird species on Earth, the Homeworld of the Knight's of the Flock. Some Squires chose legacy names, names of famous knights or family members. Some chose birds that reflected some aspect of their personality. Some still were assigned by those who simply didn't care about code names. Even still, Puffin assigned and maintained code names and more importantly identification numbers. By his account across the galaxy there were at least 1200 Puffins, none patrolled the same area, most of them had never met another Puffin and never would.

Admittedly he detested code names because his own was given as a joke in the first place. A less famous cousin to a flightless bird. The least capable member of the knight squadrons. Puffin knew that had he been born to anyone other than a ship captain in the famous Penguin family, he would not even be a knight. He'd worked to improve himself and for a time was a feared Knight in the Gaggle, under Goose. Though those days were past him. So here he was, assigning missions and tests to people that would quickly grow to out perform him.

If he had to be a puffin, he liked to imagine he'd be an alpha male puffin. He wasn't tall or short for a human, he wasn't in poor shape though his stomach did poke out slightly in ways that it didn't in his 20's. He didn't waddle when he walked. Puffin was in every sense of the word, average. He had no magic powers, he only spoke English, he could not pilot any kind of ship, he was not a berserker, or a marksman, or a swordsman. If Puffin excelled at anything, it was paperwork. Which made him perfect for his desk job.

"Sir Puffin," called out one of his Squire that had just entered his office. Puffin peered around one of the four monitors he had resting on his desk. It was Crow, a short squire with wild hair dreadlocked hair that on a good day was barely contained by a messy bun. This was not a good day. Crow had an intense glare, and a permanent frown. Crow was blessed with the unique magical ability to summon creatures at will. Crow was wearing a black cloak and a garish mask that looked like the fangs of some nightmarish creature he had probably encountered. Crow's dark brown skin was highlighted by the glow of the monitors in the dim office. Under his left eye, Crow bore a bright blue seal of mages.

"Crow," Puffin said, trying to hide the disdain in his voice. "I read in your file that you have completed 20 missions with a passing rate of one hundred percent. Though you never partner with people. Why is that?"

"Why should I?"

"Look, I didn't write the rules. You're supposed to be able to act in a group at the Squire level."

The seal under Crow's eye began glowing a bright as a golem head made up from loose paper and and office supplies around Puffin materialized on the desk.

"Yes Master." The Golem bellowed in a booming voice to Crow.

"A head." Puffin sighed, "You summoned a head"

"This head belongs to one of my Golems. I'm allowed to use them in lieu of humanoid partners."

"Doesn't matter. Your next mission requires a human partner, or an orcman, or an elf, or a dwarf or any other person. As long as they're a Squire. We need to know you can work with people."

"No." Crow said sternly.

"Yes." Puffin said returning his tone.

"On who's decree?"

"Hummingbird."

"Really? You expect me to believe Hummingbird cares what a Squire does?"

8

"Even if she didn't personally care, which she does," Puffin argued, his face turning red, "my word is the word of Hummingbird and I can remove you from your rank."

The tension in the room was dense, like a sequoia tree. Puffin shifted his gaze from Crow to the Golem's head on his desk. It's eyes darted to the back of the room.

"Can you remove your Golem's head from my desk?"

"No."

The door swung open behind Crow and in walked Raven. Normally, Puffin was tired of Raven's tardiness and over all presentation. At this exact moment, truancy was forgivable. He had after all, unintentionally prevented an altercation.

Raven was another of Puffin's least favorites. Raven was swordsman with twenty failed missions and twenty successes in the last Earth cycle.

Contrary to Crow's short stature, Raven was a large human. Nowhere near as hulking as an Orc-Man, but still over six feet tall and muscular. He was wearing a bandanna around the bottom half of his face with a black cowboy hat on his head. He didn't have any seals below his eye meaning he was magic-less. Underneath his "outlaw chic," Raven was traditionally handsome, light brown skin, perfect smile, and a chiseled jaw.

"Raven, here's your mission assignment. I'm sending you out with Crow here for a simple escort."

Raven smiled, "Sounds fun."

"You can't be serious." Crow interjected.

"Just why not?" Puffin said, he was now bored of this entire situation.

"He has a low success rate, we've all heard everything we need to know about Raven."

"Hey, what's that supposed to mean?" Raven chimed in.

"Exactly what you think." Crow growled back. "You 'save the day' but violate so many rules you may as well have stayed home. You're a Knight of the Flock not an old west cowboy."

"So you think you're better than me?" Raven took a step closer to Crow.

"You would need to get the concept of thinking to understand my answer. But yes, I'm better than you." Crow said while he looked up to Raven.

"What's that supposed to mean?"

"I can summon creatures with my thoughts. You swing a sword really hard.

Which sounds more difficult?"

"Well now, I don't want to work with you either." Raven yelled.

Puffin tapped on his desk. "Excuse me."

The arguing continued.

"Excuse me," Puffin tried again.

Puffin stood up from his chair. Puffing his chest out and deepening his voice. He yelled out, "It's not up for discussion."

The squawking Squires silenced themselves.

"Fine." They both said.

"So your mission is to an escort a Regent from Planet Aesop."

"Where are we escorting them to?" Crow said.

"It's not really an object of where but when."

"The Regent is a clairvoyant. Her specific power allegedly executes every six months in Homeworld Standard Time."

"When did it last occur?" Crow asked.

"Yesterday." Puffin replied.

Raven appeared to be deep in thought, "So what'd she see." He finally asked after an uncomfortable pause.

"She saw the two of you. I don't know the specifics beyond that. The Drakon King wants a full report of her visions and any other occurrences. Aesop is a recent integration to the Flock so we're taking these sorts of things seriously."

"So how long do I have to prepare if we have months until her next vision."

"You leave in 12 hours."

"That is nowhere near enough time." Crow complained.

"Can't do anything about it. Hummingbird's orders." Puffin said.

"That's a lie." Crow said.

"You're right." Puffin said, "They're my orders. Now get out of my office.

"

Chapter 4

Aesop was the opposite of a vacation in paradise. The planet was largely devoid of water on the surface. There were no lakes. There were no oceans. No rivers. Few, if any animals could be seen out during the day. Raven was not looking forward to his destination. He didn't need to know anything else about it. There wasn't grass or water, it was nothing like Homeworld and therefore it wouldn't be interesting to him.

The only thing he enjoyed less than going to a dried-up, desert planet was the person seated next to him on the space shuttle.

"So are you going to talk at all Crow?" Raven said after three hours in the cramped shuttle.

"I really don't see a need to." Crow said as he reclined his seat.

"Well beyond the fact that we're going to be working with each other the next six months, it's really the friendly thing to do."

"I don't care about being friendly. I don't need your help to watch one Regent."

Another three hours passed in near silence.

"So how'd you pick the name Crow?" Raven tried. Code names were a popular conversation topic among Squires. It was after all, the first defining characteristic of knighthood.

"Why did you pick Raven?" Crow asked without bothering to answer the question. Raven perked up.

"Raven was the first Black Knight. He was a just like me. Actually he was African, my grandfather was African. All descriptions of him say he had darker skin. I don't know, I just thought it would be nice to share the code name of the first human knight that looked like me."

"I can completely understand."

"So why did you pick Crow?"

"Some idiot took the name Raven from me."

Raven frowned. "Wait. Aren't you two years younger than I am?"

"Exactly. I'm not even your age and you're still a Squire. In four years, I'll probably be three ranks up on you."

"Forget that I tried talking."

"Good."

The pair sat in silence as they traveled through space. Raven imagined what it would have been like to be among the first space explorers, before Earth sent out the stations to explore neighboring star systems. He figured that they wouldn't be as bored with the experience as he was at the moment. In a way, space travel was the most beautiful thing about Raven's life. Every movie and television show got it wrong. Yes things were mostly black and white but there were occasional splashes of color and debris. It was as if they were traversing through a boundless painting.

Sometimes he would see a Star-Angel floating in the void of space as if it were a giant pink stingray in the ocean. The creatures were completely unbothered by the passing of ships or asteroids. They merely danced around any oncoming objects. They were a pure example of magic in the universe.

"Attention all passengers," the ship's A.I. said in a pleasant tone. "We are preparing for landing.

"Thank you" Raven replied politely.

"Why are you wasting your time talking to an A.I.?" Crow asked in a less than pleasant tone.

"Because A.I. have feelings too. What are you going to do during the robot uprising?"

"People have literally been predicting the robot uprising since before we first launched ships. Literally there was a small scale NRL apocalypse in 2300 in a small town in Florida. Earth has been invaded by aliens a few times. No robot uprising."

The descent was slow and loud. Raven's mother compared ship landings to airplanes on Homeworld. He always would ask if she rode on an airplane. Invariably she would say no because she was born and raised on their ship, but she had heard stories about them.

The ship landed. Immediately the passenger chamber filled with a green, lemon scented gas that made it possible for all passengers to speak the native language and breathe the air on the new planet. Raven wasn't sure what the gas was called, just that it was magical in origin. Knights typically called it Translation Mist. Once they had breathed enough in, the ship doors opened. Raven stood up, grabbed his swords and strapped them to his waist.

The katana was mostly just for show, the beam sword was his real weapon. It was designed to slice through most solid materials as long as they weren't magical in origin. The handle was made of Dark Star, a magical material designed for weapons. Goblins famously used dark star weapons in a war with humans during the Iron Age. How they acquired a ritual magic spell was beyond Raven's imagination. Dark Star was nowhere near as useful as Blood Star, but to obtain Blood Star, Raven would need to perform a Blood Magic ritual and those were barred by anyone that wasn't a full fledged Knight.

Raven wondered what, if anything, Crow would bring on a mission. Did he have a grimoire? A wand? A magic staff? He'd seen every one of those tools used by mages before but Crow wasn't brandishing anything of the sort.

The pair of Squires exited the ship. Before they realized how hot it actually was, they walked immediately into an elevator that sunk into the ground.

Chapter 5

Crow had been annoyed from the moment they learned of the mission. His first moment of relief came when he met the Regent's bodyguards as soon as they stepped off the elevator. The guard was someone's Golem. His eyes lit up as he immediately walked past everything around him straight to the guard.

The Golem was around seven feet tall. It was made of stone but it had eyes made of jade. What impressed Crow the most were the details on the Golem. It had small details carved into it, finger nails, muscles, it's face was capable of expression. This would have been difficult for even a master to make.

Beside the Golem was the Regent's bodyguard. She wasn't as exciting for Crow to look at. She had the characteristic pink skin and purple eyes of a subsurface dweller of Aesop. Underneath her left eye was the Blue Seal of a mage that was indicative of all the mages in the Kingdom. She had jet black hair. While she was thin, she looked healthy rather than the starved appearance of some of the people known to come from Aesop. Her face betrayed her thoughts as she was clearly frustrated by something. Both she and the Golem could be identified as part of the Regent's court by the symbol of the planet Aesop, pinned to their chest.

"Ma'am." Crow said to the Regent's bodyguard without taking his eyes off the Golem.

"You have got to be kidding me. These can not be Knights of the Flock." The bodyguard said plainly.

"Why is that?" Raven asked. Crow remained silent.

"Well you're dressed like a Earth Old West Cowboy. And he's just, not as tall as I suspected."

"I'm still taller than you," Crow said under his breath.

"Whatever you say little man." The Regent's bodyguard replied. "Come on, we're off to see the Regent."

"Wait," Raven said, "I thought we were supposed to be meeting the Regent here?"

"Oh no. Gods no." The bodyguard laughed out. Crow looked at both the bodyguard and Raven. He was disappointed in his situation.

As they walked past the large room the elevator exited into and started through Aesop's underground city-state, Atlas, Crow grew on edge. He couldn't appreciate the beauty of the city which was made of domed buildings bathed in a blue light. The light made the Aesopians appear purple as they passed by the group.

The people themselves were all easily identifiable. They wore pins on their chest that depicted their job role. The only people not wearing pins were children. Everyone was thin. Most were taller than Crow.

"So who summoned the Golem?" Crow asked.

"He's not summoned, I brought him to life."

"So you're a Mage?" Raven interrupted.

"I wouldn't call myself a Mage." The bodyguard said, "I just know magic."

"Well then what do we call you bodyguard?" Raven asked.

"Kiva." The bodyguard said, "yourselves?"

"I'm Raven and this is Crow."

"So I have to ask. Why aren't you wearing the suits of armor that we see on all the ads?"

"Common misconception." Crow answered.

"Explain."

"The suits of armor are only for formal events, generals, the kings guard. They have a protection spell but it only works under very specific conditions." Crow explained.

"Plus, they're super heavy." Raven chimed in. "Usually you'll see us wearing our light armors like we have on now. A lot of knights will wear clothes over them too. Plus we get to pick the color of our light armors and they have minor protection spells on them."

The group passed by a shop selling magical artifacts. Under normal circumstances it would be Crow's job to run an inspection for anything that might be considered dangerous. He stared at the shop.

"Detect level three dangers among us." He whispered to himself as Raven told a story about how he once had been stuck in his armor for three days after a ceremony he attended. As expected the store itself glowed red to Crow alone. Though that only meant something in the shop was classified as level three or higher. He wouldn't know what it was without going inside. Unsurprisingly the Golem that they were walking with was also glowing red. Raven was carrying something dangerous as well but he would be permitted.

What did surprise Crow was that nothing else was glowing. Level three magic was a common misdemeanor. A lot of times, people had level three without meaning to. He looked around again, nothing. He'd leave it to local authorities.

"Detect level four." He whispered to himself.

The Golem still glowed. Crow assumed that parts of it would probably reach all the way up to level six. This would allow Kiva to disassemble it, or shrink it whenever needed. At least, that's what Crow would do if he weren't a summoner.

The hilts of Raven's swords were glowing. They must have had some sort of spell on them to prevent his arm getting cut off in a duel. The shop still glowed. Anyone that walked out of the shop was glowing. Kiva started glowing.

The group was starting to walk past the area where the shop would be detected.

"Everyone stop."

"Why?" Raven asked in a slightly annoyed tone. Crow didn't care that he interrupted the details of Raven getting cut from his armor. Kiva gave Crow a look that was what Crow assumed was gratitude.

"Raven, do you know what moves a misdemeanor to a felony for magical objects."

"Of course I do. Non permitted individuals carrying a single level four or higher item. A shop selling level five or higher items. Anyone including Knights, Squires, and Royal Guard carrying or selling level ten."

"The shop is at least selling level four and I can't think of a single reason why anyone on Aesop needs a permit." Crow said.

"I'm carrying level seven magic, but I have permits. Do you need to see my license?" Kiva answered.

"Not right now. You missed my point," Crow said, "That shop is dealing illegal magical equipment. I guarantee it."

"Can you prove it."

"Share my magical vision," Crow cast a spell enabling Raven and Kiva to see anything he could only see because of magic. He was only speaking his spells for the comfort of those around him.

"Wow." Raven said, "Do mages see like this all the time?"

"No." Kiva and Crow answered at the same time. Crow wondered if she was just as annoyed with Raven as he was.

"Detect level five." Crow cast.

The shop was still glowing.

"Raven. We need to go check this out."

"But our mission." Raven said. His eyes grew wide.

"I can't return to the ship knowing that there's a dealer on a planet with almost no magical defense. Neither should you."

"I'll make this easier for you." Kiva said. "I'm going too."

"No you're not."

"If you don't let me, I can't bring you to the Regent."

Crow audibly sighed then marched into the store. Everything seemed to be in order. It had the standard wall of cards which were used to summon objects from another realm to this plane. Of course there were physical objects as well to entice shoppers. What caught Crow's eye was the counter, the shop keeper, and the wall behind him were all glowing.

"Good evening friends." The shop keeper asked, "is there anyway that I can help a couple loyal Knights of the Flock."

"We were just in the neighborhood." Raven said, "thought we'd see what all you have."

The shop keeper started sweating profusely.

"Is there anything you're specifically looking for though?"

"No." Crow said. He was trying to make himself more intimidating by intentionally allowing his magical power "leak" so that everyone in the vicinity could feel it. Then the unexpected happened.

Chapter 6

Abead of sweat fell from Raven's forehead. The shopkeeper was hurling some sort of ice magic at them. Unlike Crow and Kiva, Raven had no magical ability, so while they were able to deflect the spells, he needed to dodge them. The floor around him was a sheet of ice. As were the walls behind him.

Crow had made some sort of magic bubble around himself. Somehow the ice spells went through Kiva. Raven was at once jealous that he was not magically gifted. Next he was glad that he was wearing a hat and coat.

It was safe to say that the shopkeeper was not going to turn himself in. Perhaps Raven should have let Crow talk through the situation. Instead, Raven decided to tackle the shopkeeper and hold him down to the floor.

Raven dodged another ice spell. Unfortunately, it hit his hat, causing the collector's item to shatter like a dropped tea cup.

"Damnit that was one of a kind. I can't get another one."

"It was a stupid hat anyway." Crow said.

"It was not stupid. It was a Homeworld item. I bought it custom from a small store that hand stitches everything. If I order another one it won't arrive for six years. Unless I win the lottery or something. Ugh."

A shard of ice whizzed past Raven's ear. The shopkeeper was using a magic staff to shoot ice spells in random directions with little, if any, control. It was apparent that the shopkeeper definitely did not have a license for items that produced attack spells.

Raven figured if he could get close enough to the staff without getting blasted by an ice spell, he could slice the staff in half.

"Whatever you're thinking, stop it," Crow said as Raven tightened his grip on his sword.

"I would rather not." Raven replied.

Kiva's Golem rushed past both of the Squires and pinned the shop keeper to the floor.

"You two need to be more concerned with the threat than each other." Kiva barked at them.

This statement obviously ruffled Crow's feathers.

"Why don't you shut your mouth and use that Golem of yours to contain the perpetrator." Crow shouted.

Raven sliced through a block of ice as Crow summoned about thirty flying hands that all attacked the shopkeeper. Raven charged in to grab or slice the magic staff but was instead sent flying back. Kiva's Golem picked up a table and swung it at the shop keeper's head.

The table cracked in half but the shopkeeper was still standing. A sheet of ice covered the shopkeeper. Spikes of ice began to sprout from his back. He appeared to be in pain.

"Damnit" Crow cursed.

"What is happening?" Kiva asked.

"He's lost control of the magical object."

"So, what's going to happen to him?" Raven asked while slicing through a flying chunk of ice. The flying ice was getting larger. Raven was doing his best to cut the ice.

"I WILL NOT GO DOWN EASY. I AM NOT TURNING ITSELF IN TO THE KNIGHTS," The Shopkeeper wailed as a blast of cold air ripped through the shop. What wasn't frozen, was destroyed. The shop was ruined.

This was the risk of abusing magic. A Nought. As in their humanity was for nought. Raven had never actually seen a Nought in person, but he had learned enough about them in the academy and in reports that he knew he was looking at an Ice Nought. It was like a walking ice statue with spikes jutting out of its titanic fists and legs. Mist and water fell from it's body as it was clearly not supposed to be in their current climate, let alone this plane of existence.

"Raven." Crow said, "do you know what we're looking at?"

"That is a Nought." Raven said, "we need to take care of it before it starts growing."

Kiva's Golem kicked the Nought in the chest and into the wall.

"I don't suppose either of you know fire magic?" Kiva yelled at the Squires as she took a glancing blow from a chunk of ice the size of a reclining chair.

The Ice Nought took a gigantic labored step toward the group. Cold air blasted them. Raven felt the hair on his face freeze in place. The Nought was now unrecognizable as any sort of human creature. It was covered in hundreds of spikes and thick layers of ice. It was already larger than the shopkeeper was and still growing.

Raven used his sword to cut off the Nought's head. For a moment everything was still. Then a blast of cold air signaled that the fight was far from over. The Nought's grew back, this time with a crown of spikes.

Raven paused. He didn't know if there was a way to disable the Nought. If they gave up, they could retreat and get help.

Kiva's Golem punched a hole through the Nought's chest and stuck itself in place. The Nought let out a wail. It couldn't move. It was trapped by the much heavier golem.

"Now's my chance." Crow said. He sprinted into the path of the thrashing Nought and placed his hand on its chest.

The Nought began to disappear into Crow's hand as if it were a vacuum.

"Why didn't you open with that move?" Raven yelled at Crow. Raven was genuinely upset.

"I couldn't. I just absorbed him into a tiny magical door and stored him in my dimension. I wouldn't be allowed to do that if he had any type of humanity left. Otherwise we'd have had to kill him."

"So what happens to him now?"

"Now, he becomes one of my summons, after he makes a contract with Numcustos for his services. Don't worry, you'll see him again."

"Who's Numcustos?" Raven asked.

"Not important at the moment." Crow replied.

"Good, so we can meet someone actually important then," Kiva interrupted, "now it's time for you to meet the Regent."

"Wait, when are we going to see the Nought again?" Raven asked.

"Don't worry about it."

"Maybe we should be worried," Kiva said. Her Golem was picking itself up and scraping ice off of its chest. The shop was ruined. Raven and Crow picked up every illegal item level six or higher. One such item was a staff of fire. Raven was very glad that shopkeeper used the ice staff instead.

"Do you mind if local authorities do the rest of the clean up?" Kiva asked in a slightly annoyed tone.

"Honestly, we'd probably prefer it." Crow answered back. "Local crime is not really our job. We just aren't allowed to ignore it either."

Raven did not prefer the local authorities getting credit. He was struggling not to go back to the ship and report this turn of events to Puffin. It wasn't against the Knights of the Flock's code of ethics to capture magical beasts, but this one in particular was an intelligent life form. Raven didn't know what to do.

So he did nothing.

Walking out of the store was an interesting experience. It was as if nobody knew what had just happened. This was why Raven was not enamored with the idea of dealing with magic, the rule seemed olyto exist to non-mages. They walked another couple miles through the busy town hub before reaching the Regent's home. The Mansion was surrounded by guards in white space armor. Each guard's face was obscured by a visor that made their pink skin appear dark purple. They each were armed with plasma cannons. A few of the guards had beam swords.

Raven's mind wandered to the kinds of training that Aesopians would be able to do. He wondered if they did their training underground with society or in the harsh environment of the surface. How skilled were the swordsmen of the Regent's Guard? The question rang through his mind over and over as he stared at them.

The group walked into the mansion and stood in the foyer. It was a large area with a flight of stairs on the left side. The walls were adorned with expensive looking paintings. Above them was a large gold chandelier. The floor was an immaculate stone. Raven felt almost guilty standing inside the mansion wearing his usual uniform. Guilty wasn't the right word. He had done nothing wrong. He felt poor.

A man with fuchsia skin and antennae wearing a perfectly creased gray suit walked down the stairs. He had a smug expression about himself that made Raven aware that this was not his world.

"Now presenting The Drakon King's chosen Regent of Aesop, Mirai," the man said in as dry a tone as Raven expected.

Mirai was not what Raven predicted. She was shorter than Crow. Her skin was a light shade of pink, just slightly too pink to be mistaken for an earthling. She had both ears and antennae which seemed to be a bit of an oddity among the Aesopians, whom as far as raven could tell had either or. Raven wondered if she had extra hearing. Mirai was wearing a black uniform with a protective vest covering it. Her face was round with flawless skin highlighted by a glowing blue mage seal under her left eye. This was not the regal woman that was described in the file.

"Your Regency." Crow said while bowing. Raven bowed immediately following Crow.

Mirai stared at the knights. "Um. Who are you again?" Mirai said. "Veelinkiva, who did you bring here?"

"These are the Knights of the Flock that you saw in your vision your Regency" Kiva answered.

"I know that Veelinkiva. I mean, who are they?"

The way Mirai stressed every syllable in "Veelinkiva" was jovial as if she was intentionally trying to provoke her bodyguard.

"The tall one is Raven." Kiva said, "The other one is Crow."

"The pleasure is all yours I'm sure." Mirai said.

Chapter 7

Crow had been annoyed from the moment he set foot on Aesop. He grew frustrated that even on an alien planet he felt superior. That nobody was on his level of magic understanding. He was forced to capture the Nought because the shopkeeper was an idiot that didn't understand magic. Now he stood in front of The Drakon King's chosen Regent for this planet, and she couldn't be bothered to remember his name, or even why he was there.

They had migrated from the entrance way to an office. The room had a dark blue carpet. Paintings of Aesopians adorned the walls. The only portrait that wasn't of an Aesopian was of a man with a well-kept beard, square glasses, and an intense glare. Underneath the man's left eye was a golden mage seal. The portrait of The Drakon King stood out like a sore thumb, yet made perfect sense given the room's aesthetics.

Crow was impressed with the room. This did not mitigate his frustration. He wondered if anyone could tell his emotions. If Edgor the butler had any emotional intelligence, Crow would have been surprised. Kiva, however, had made eye contact with Crow more than once during their explanation of what happened to the only magical item vendor in the town surrounding the mansion.

"So where is he?" Mirai asked.

"As I said, your regency," Crow replied, "he's in another dimension."

"The Home for Infinite Losers?" Mirai asked causing Raven to laugh.

"No madam." Crow said out loud while thinking that he was surrounded by idiots.

"Never mind. I really don't care anymore." Mirai said.

Crow sighed. The Regent was nowhere near the level of intelligence that would be required for a magical trait like clairvoyance. They were assigned a mission with no specific purpose. It was a set up. No matter what they did, this mission would be a guaranteed failure.

"This mission is not a failure. That's what you're getting ready to go and complain about once Edgor shows you to your room."

Crow stopped everything he was doing. The Regent's file said nothing about her being a telepath.

"I'm not a telepath. I can read your immediate future." Mirai said, "oh the file only talks about the long-term thing. I legitimately have visions every hour, it's a side effect of my own time magic. Sometimes multiple if I'm shifted in just the right way. Every six months, I report to The Drakon King because those are just the biggest in scale. I'm sure The Drakon King doesn't want hear about a vision, about the vision, I had about tacos. Why do you look so confused?"

"The file we got dramatically undersold your abilities." Crow said.

Mirai paused, "There's a clairvoyant and you honestly thought all the information about them would be in the file. You're silly."

"Can you tell me my future?" Raven interrupted.

"Isn't that why you're ultimately here?" Mirai said as she threw her head back.

"Your Regency, we were assigned to guard you until your next major vision." Crow said, "We aren't here to get our futures read."

"Not really though. You're Squires. If they really wanted to protect me, a Regent and a Clairvoyant, they'd have sent members of The Gaggle or even The Charm. They might have even sent Royal Guard."

Crow hadn't thought about that aspect of his mission. Squires were usually only given guard duty for short periods of time or major events. This was a major assignment. Why wouldn't they have assigned one of the members of three of the most equipped Knight Squads?

"So why did you request us? Are we some chosen ones for a prophecy."

"No. But you do keep appearing in my visions. What I do know is the two of you are going to have three fights, years apart. I don't know why. But for some reason I'm there for all three. Sometimes I'm there. Sometimes I'm in a ship nearby. But I'm always there. It looks like we're stuck together." She poked Crow in the chest, "Sometimes you die. Sometimes you don't. Sometimes he's more of a monster than anything you've ever seen. Sometimes he's your closest friend.

There's a lot of different possible futures, but I see you two a lot and it always ends in the three fights."

Crow frowned. He'd be dealing with Raven for years. There was no way to avoid it. Until this point, he had thought that everything that happened was a reflection of choice. He had an internalized tantrum; this could not be the way that things were. Crow was not going to accept that his life was completely predetermined. He looked at Raven whom seemed perfectly content knowing the future. No, he didn't seem content knowing, he was content. It was infuriating.

"So when you see the future, is it an exact thing or is there room for interpretation." Crow asked.

"It's more like I can see an exact action at an unknown point in the future. Think of it like a video game with cutscenes that will always occur no matter what choices you make in the game some things will be different but the big actions will always be the same. There are always going to be people that put those scenes off as long as possible. If I told you, you were going to die soon, you might go insane trying to prevent it. You might prolong your life, but eventually you'd die. Everyone does, even vampires. They go extinct eventually."

"Your Regency!" Edgor chimed in.

"Oh I'm sorry, I'm not supposed to mention extinction level events. In fact, new rule, anything you say or hear with me is to be kept secret. Am I clear?"

To Crow, none of this was clear. Regardless, he agreed.

"So why did you hire Kiva?"

"I had a vision that she will be in a room when I'm in a meeting with The Drakon King and she will be made a Knight of the Flock."

"Which I've always said was impossible because I never attended an academy nor became a Squire." Kiva said, "Now I'm an adult, it's too late. Yet here I am protecting the Regent from a threat that never comes. For an apparent chance at an impossible dream."

"But you love being here." Mirai said.

"Regrettably." Kiva replied. Q

"That's enough future talk ma'am." Edgor chimed in, "I'm sure your new guards are hungry."

Crow was famished. He along with Kiva and Raven followed Edgor to a lavish dining hall. The food however seemed alien. The gilded table and soft chairs were betrayed by giant insects, a gelatinous substance with bubbles floating over it, glasses of dark pink liquid, and some sort of green meat.

"Crow, I don't want to eat it." Raven complained. It was the first thing they had ever agreed upon.

"Is there something wrong with our delicacies here?" Edgor asked in an intimidating tone.

"They're Earthlings." Kiva answered before Crow could think of an excuse, "perhaps something that more aligns with Earth cuisine."

"No this is fine." Crow said as he scooped a spoonful of the gelatin into his mouth. This was an immediate mistake. The gelatin was so spicy that he could feel his forehead break into a cold sweat before he even swallowed. Every single book on interplanetary etiquette had lied, eating local cuisine did not make him feel more worldly at the moment. He needed to drink something. He grabbed his glass of the pink liquid. It did not help.

"Are you okay?" Kiva asked.

"Water." Crow coughed out.

Raven reached into his coat pocket and tossed Crow a bottle of water. Crow drank the whole thing without question. For a brief moment, water was the greatest thing that Crow had ever tasted.

Edgor looked at Raven and Crow in disgust and walked away. Before he exited the restaurant, he looked back and said, "if you wanted food from home so bad you may as well just go to the Earth restaurant down the street. You're honestly as disappointing as The Drakon King."

Once Edgor had walked out of the room, Kiva looked at Raven and Crow and said, "grab your stuff we're going to eat Earth food."

"So where are we going?" Mirai said from the doorway that Edgor had just marched out of.

"Your Regency, we're just going to get Earth food as Raven and Crow can't quite stomach our cuisine."

"That makes sense. Whenever The Drakon King visits he can't handle the food either, it must be an Earth thing. Kiva, can you have that Golem of yours carry my bag."

"You're coming?" Kiva replied.

"Can you think of a reason that I shouldn't?"

"No." Kiva answered.

"Then dinner's on me." Mirai shouted as she handed her bag to the Golem.

Chapter 8

They were in a chain restaurant. The wait staff were all poorly built robots. The robots themselves had the characteristic giant faces of the Metal Face machines from planet DOOM. Though they were nowhere near as clean as DOOM's machines, Raven still liked their appearance.

The only humanoid working seemed to be a thin Aesopian with antennae that we're slightly too long for his bright pink face. The group were seated in a booth far from the rest of the patrons. On the wall to their left was a television airing some sort of Earth sports.

Raven wondered if this were live tv that he was watching or if it were on the standard tape delay of five years. It wasn't of high importance.

Raven took a bite of his mozzarella sticks. At some point in the past, before people learned to cook with magic, he'd have had to worry about caloric intake and other values that he didn't have time for. Now, it was just about the feeling of cheese moving around his mouth. Mozzarella sticks in the age of The Drakon King were a perfect blend of science and magic. Sadly, this was one of few examples as the two worlds still clashed often.

Next to him was Kiva whom had ordered some sort of pasta dish, albeit covered in an Aesopian spice. Crow was sitting across from Raven, he was eating grilled chicken. Next to Crow, Mirai had ordered one of everything on the menu. This was excessive to say the least, but she seemed to be content taking a bite or two from each dish and passing the plate back or to anyone at the table that wanted the remainder.

"So, let's play a game." Mirai said after a small sip of chicken soup.

"What would you like to play, Your Regency." Crow replied.

"The next person at this table to refer to me as Your Regency or any other official title shall be reprimanded harshly. You may call me Mirai."

"Understood, Mirai." The three guards replied in unison.

"Much better." Mirai said through a smile. "The game is truth or truth. We would play truth or dare, except Edgor would have you all killed if I came home with so much as a split end. So who's going to start?"

Raven, Crow, and Kiva grew silent. Raven couldn't tell if the Regent had been joking or not. This was certainly not noble behavior.

"Fine. I'll start." Mirai said, "Raven. Truth or truth?"

"Truth," Raven answered.

"Why do you wear cowboy hats and bandannas?"

Raven breathed a sigh of relief, an easy question. "To look like some of my favorite characters in books. Before you ask, yes, I know it looks stupid. I just like it."

"Great. Your turn. Pick someone." Mirai said.

"Crow."

"No."

"Play along or you could get a bad report." Mirai said almost teasingly.

"Fine." Crow said through clenched teeth.

"What's your family like?"

"My father is The Drakon King's personal advisor..." Crow started.

"Wait which one?" Raven interrupted.

"Tempest."

Crow was a noble. Crow was an elf. Crow was the son of a Royal Advisor. Suddenly Raven understood why Crow had an air of superiority about him.

"No more interruptions." Mirai said while batting her eyes. "If you're a noble, you're suddenly husband material. So who's your mother?"

"Trust me, I'm not a noble." Crow said, "My mother was The Resolution 1's Magic Director."

Crow was only half elf. Raven wondered which he identified as.

"Kiva." Crow said.

"Sure." Kiva said.

"How long does it take you to build a Golem?"

"About a year." Kiva answered, "Crow."

"Let me guess. Same question."

"No." Kiva retorted, "Where's your favorite place to go?"

"I don't know. For a vacation, I went to Absoul last year. In everyday life, my workshop."

"Mirai" Crow said.

"Yes"

"How did you become a Regent?"

"I had a vision that The Drakon King was standing outside while it was raining blood when I was a little girl. Six months later at the Battle for COROT 7B, The Drakon King debuted his Crimson Rain spell and killed every living thing on the battlefield. My father told the former Regent about it and was beheaded. Then the Regent took me to meet The Drakon King. When it came out that I was more or less a slave, The Drakon King killed the Regent and put me in his place. Our only condition for joining the Flock was that we had to end slavery there and then."

Raven sympathized with Mirai. His own father was killed for being a whistleblower about a corrupt ship captain. He started to say something but instead was chosen to answer her next question.

"Where did you grow up?"

"I grew up on The Resolution 1 then The Resolution 2. I've never lived on a Planet before." Raven answered, "Crow."

"What?"

"What do you think we're going to fight over?"

"Honest answer. You're an idiot that has beyond all conceivable reason been able to maintain your status as a member of the Knights of the Flock. For all I know, you're going to crack under the pressure and I'll have to reign you in."

Raven felt like he had been punched in the chest. He was not as adept a knight as Crow, but he was by no means an idiot. Here he was questioning his motives. He stopped eating his mozzarella sticks. As a child if someone would have said something like that, Raven would have started crying. While he was angered, it wasn't an urge to cry that filled him. Instead, it was a feeling of resolve.

Raven was going to say something when Kiva stood up and shouted out, "That was terrible. Apologize to him now."

A stone hand reached out and slapped Crow across the face. Crow sat in apparent shock. For a moment the room was silence. Then the silence was broken by Mirai's laughter.

"Kiva. I don't need to see the future to know that he's going to be thinking about that all night."

Raven choked down a laugh. Despite how generally terrible Crow has been on this mission, they would need to coexist for the next six months. It wasn't worth risking failure by alienating himself from his fellow Squire any further. Oddly, Raven felt himself beginning to appreciate Crow as a person. Crow was abrasive, but he was honest.

When they finished. They returned to the mansion, ignored the glares from Edgor and went to bed.

Chapter 9

Six weeks into the current round of missions, Puffin felt the need to do some evaluations of how the Squires were all doing. He sat at his desk behind his computer monitors and sipped through a comically large cup of coffee. Between sips he would open the reports on the screens.

The first report he read was about his cousin, Penguin. Penguin was leading a small unit of Squires on an exploratory mission on a recently discovered gas giant. Apparently, Penguin had captured some sort of indigenous life form that had attacked the crew of the ship she was on then determined that it was intelligent enough to negotiate it's placement in the Flock. Certainly, she would be awarded. Puffin was simultaneously proud and jealous. She was off gallivanting about the universe and he was filing her exploits into a database. Regardless Penguin had earned the right to take the Test of Might.

The next report was about a Dwarf code named Condor. Condor was perhaps the first known Dwarven Mage. Because of his unique ability, his missions were generally peace keeping between the Dwarven colonies on Venus. Condor would be a valuable asset in Drakon Kingdom-Dwarven relations if he passed the Test of Might. The Dwarves referred to him as their "first wizard."

A three-person team of Ostrich, Swallow, and Cassowary were on an escort mission with a Regent on a trip from planet to planet. Teleportation magic being outlawed made assigning missions easier than ever. A group like Ostrich and his compatriots were better suited for war. Puffin couldn't wait to see how they did in the Test of Might.

A message appeared on screen from Edgor, attendant to Mirai, Regent of Aesop. Crow and Raven had surprisingly done well. Though the message noted that both were picky eaters. Puffin laughed out loud. Raven and Crow were able to coexist long enough for a positive report.

Puffin reached down for his mug and took a long, satisfied sip. As the liquid warmed him from the inside out. He felt a fleeting happiness that he had a complete group of Squires ready or almost ready to become Knights of the Flock.

That's when he heard a loud banging at his door. This was strange, there shouldn't have been anyone on his floor with all the Squires out and about. He stood up and turned off his monitors.

"Who's there." Puffin called out.

There was no answer. Puffin started to sit down. Then there was another banging at the door.

Puffin reached under his desk and picked up a beam sword. He flipped the switch and turned it on. The blade was dark blue and vibrating. The vibration wasn't a good sign. The blade likely had a dying battery from being over charged.

He pressed the button on his desk to open the door. Light flooded the room from the hallway. Nobody was there. Puffin walked into the hallway and looked in both directions.

Suddenly he felt a sharp pain in his left thigh. Something had tried to shoot him with some sort of spell.

Tried was the operative word. For years, Puffin had been compensating for his lack of magical defense by drinking from mugs with runes of protection etched into the bottom. He could get hit with hundreds of spells and never experience more than beyond mild physical pain. Unless it was a significant spell he would never have known. Regardless, he couldn't see any assailant. He would never be able to defeat an enemy of this level.

Another sharp pain, this one in the middle of his spine. They were fast. The first attack clearly came from in front. The second came from behind. He needed to call for help. The opponent was too fast. Puffin drew and carelessly started swinging his sword around.

A yelp penetrated the silence of his opponent. He still couldn't seem them. He didn't know what kind of magic this was but they were invisible and almost intangible. They made no sound when they moved. All of a sudden there was a sharp pain in his chest. He fell to the ground as he looked at a pool of his own blood.

Chapter 10

Magical alerts were a form of teleportation magic. Unlike teleportation of humankind, this required no actual sacrifice as life energy was not required for the spell's activation. Technology was by far the easier way to send a message even across planets, though a magical alert was by far the most secure. A magical message could not be ignored. Once received the message would repeat until a reply was sent. For this reason alone, Magical Alerts were only ever sent between mages that were part of the Knights of the Flock. Unbeknownst to Crow and Raven, they were going to receive one such message.

Crow and Raven were seated at a table as Kiva and Mirai were eating some sort of Aesopian delicacy. Weeks ago, Crow would have at least tried it. However he gave up eating anything Aesopian after the ninth or tenth failed experience. While Mirai tried several different desserts until she made a choice, Crow felt his eyes start burning. He balled a fist and started rubbing them.

Kiva must have noticed Crow rubbing his eyes.

"Did you eat the food again?" she asked in a scolding tone.

"No" Crow barked back.

"Let me see it," Raven said, "I have a medical pack. You might have some sort of infection."

Before Crow could deny Raven, his fellow Squire was holding open his eyelids with one hand and attempting to put eyedrops his eyes with the other.

As the drop made contact with Crow's pupil Raven was pushed back by a large white viscous fluid mass flying out of Crow's eye. The mass bubbled and began to take shape. After a few moments the mass could be identified as a swan.

"What is that?" Kiva said as the swan walked around the dining room.

"It's a bird." Raven replied.

"I see that." Kiva said in response, "What's it doing here."

"It's a message from Lady Swan of the Gaggle." Crow said, clutching his eye.

"What's it say?"

"I don't know." Crow replied. He had never had to interpret a Magical Alert before.

"So how do we get the message?"

"The message cannot be spread with creatures that do not fly with the Flock." The swan spoke in a clear, confident woman's voice.

"I'm sorry Mirai, Kiva." Crow said.

The Aesopians left the room. The Swan marched around the area, turning its head back and forth as if inspecting the area. Once it was finished, it waddled to Crow's feet and started speaking.

"Crow, first tier Squire, and all accompanying Knights of the Flock. This is a message from Lieutenant Swan of the Gaggle. Note that any orders that you receive come with the authority of Knight Commander Goose of the Gaggle."

Crow looked at Raven. He couldn't tell if the other Squire could grasp the situation.

The Swan continued, "All Squires and Lower Ranked Knights are required to return to your home ships. If you are on a bodyguard mission, your charge and any of their staff will have the option to return to the ship with you."

The Swan disappeared and flew back into Crow's eye. Crow winced as he thought about the message they just received.

"Wait, what just happened?" Raven asked. He had a look of bewilderment on his face.

"Swan summoned a familiar through my Mage's crest to deliver a message."

"No. I get that part." Raven said, "I want to know why?"

"I don't know." Crow answered.

"The only reason they'd call us back would be because something happened. It wasn't a 'Crow and Raven come back' message it was an 'everyone return now' message.

Crow wondered to himself about the events that led to that situation. A total return of both Squires and Low Ranks meant there was some sort of danger that could affect the whole Flock. The last total return of all Knights was fifty years ago when it was discovered that vampirism was not a Homeworld-exclusive condition. Since then, Vampire combat was a mandatory course that all cadets took on the ship regardless of whether or not they became Knights. While total returns of Squires were more common, they weren't as frequently included with other Knight Tiers. Regardless of why they were being called back, Crow was positive that the discovery had to be on this level.

Chapter 11

Raven loved Mirai's personal space cruiser. Their journey back to The Resolution was much more comfortable than their journey to Aesop had been. Though the second they took off, he knew that Mirai and possibly Kiva would be disappointed in ship life. There would be no more lavish dinners, or butlers, or people to do laundry for them. They would be responsible for themselves. Raven was going to miss the small glimpse he got into the life of nobility.

Before exiting the cruiser, the group was washed with the familiar green gas so that they would all be speaking the same language. As the doors opened Raven's jaw dropped at the scene before him. Every Squire and low tier knight was in the docking bay. Ships and cruisers were arriving every few seconds. It looked more like a high traffic airport than a mobile base of operation.

Androids walking around the area began greeting dignitaries that had decided to remain with their assigned knights. Within a few minutes the androids and the nobility had left the docking bay completely leaving only the Knights of the Flock standing waiting for orders.

Thirty minutes passed. Nobody spoke a word. Raven wondered what would happen next. Beside him, Crow was watching the overhead monitors intently. The monitors had stopped showing flight information and instead had switched to a live feed of the docking bay.

An hour passed. Raven noticed a few, newer squires grab their belongings and start making their way to the exits, only to be stopped by androids. Raven elected not to move.

An android appeared on the live feed. It wasn't cracked like its contemporaries. This one had a silver, shiny body, and an arm cannon. Painted on the android's chest was a golden dragon with its mouth open.

"Attention all, attention. Please welcome his honorable King of the Empire..." Raven stopped listening. He didn't need to hear the long introduction. They all knew who it was. This was The Drakon King. His list of feats was beyond compare to any Knight of the Flock. He was the first mage to build a nuclear fusion engine with magic. He was the one that ended the Vampire War. He brokered the peace between Orc-Elves and Elves. He was the Knight of the Flock born to common blood that became King. He was everyone's hero.

Every Squire, Knight, and remaining civilian in the room kneeled on one knee. Most of the Squires were smiling, some were crying tears of joy at seeing The Drakon King. For a Squire to see The Drakon King was such an immense honor that most never imagined it would happen. Raven was taking mental notes of everything happening so that he could write this experience in a journal later. Raven was not a frequent journal writer. Conversely, Crow seemed unbothered.

"Hello." The Drakon King spoke. His voice had a youthful tone that was betrayed by his gray hair and beard. Other than that, he looked like he sounded. Had he wanted to, he could have been a movie star, or a model of some sort. Every hair in place, his suit was perfect. His skin was a perfect golden brown. A common joke about The Drakon King was that he was the one human that even Orcs were attracted to, Raven could see why.

"Before I begin, I want to tell you that I read each and every one of your files. I am impressed. So impressed that I would like to commend a few of you."

The Drakon King walked around the room. He patted a few of the kneeling Squires on the head without saying anything. Then he stopped in front of Raven.

"Rise, Raven." The Drakon King spoke. Raven stood up as quickly as he could.

The Drakon King places his hand on Raven's shoulder. "This Squire has, to scale, the highest failure percentage in the room."

Raven's heart sank. A few people in the crowd laughed.

"Do you know why he has failed missions?" The Drakon King asked the Crowd.

The crowd didn't answer.

"Because Raven does more for the greater good than the parameters of the mission. Like some of you in this room, Raven has no magical abilities. Unlike most of you though, he hasn't let a weakness hinder his progress. I read a letter about Raven taking on an entire horde of NRLs for five days by himself while waiting for help to arrive. Yes, the farm he was hired to protect was destroyed, but not one person died."

The laughter stopped.

"In another report, Raven was fired from his mission because he refused to leave a sick child behind while guarding a caravan on a three-planet tour."

Raven wasn't sure which happened first, smiling or crying. Regardless he was a mess.

"Even recently, Raven charged into battle against an Ice Nought, knowing that he had no way to defeat it on his own." The Drakon King continued, "Not your brightest move Squire." Raven laughed with the crowd.

"Raven, remain standing," The Drakon King said as he took one step to his left, "Rise Crow."

"Crow has never failed a mission. Never even come close." The Drakon King said to gasps in the crowd. "More than that, until the mission he is currently on. He did them all by himself. That's over twenty straight successes with no team. There are some of you in groups of five that would fail your current missions if I didn't recall."

"Remain standing."

"Rise Penguin" A shorter woman stood up. She was muscular but still feminine in appearance. She had brown curly hair, and a gaze that could kill. This was Raven's best friend from the Academy. She stood up as the King put a hand on her shoulder. Raven was happy that she was receiving praise.

"Penguin is maybe the best leader in the room, myself included," The Drakon King said, "Maybe not quite better than me." The Drakon King laughed, the crowd laughed.

"Many of you have been in operations led by Squire Penguin. Yes, even Knights. I had the opportunity to oversee a project led by her. Penguin was able to have multiple teams explore and terraform an uninhabited moon. She also shot a bolt through the skull of a Vampire that was clinging to the Cruiser she was on when it landed. If it wasn't for her, I might be the Vampire King right now."

The Drakon King laughed again. The crowd also laughed though less enthusiastically.

The Drakon King stepped away from Penguin. "I didn't come here to praise you for your individual accomplishments. I came here to tell you what great thing you're doing next. Your next challenge will be a Test of Might. Low Tier Knights will also have a test."

The Drakon King started walking around the area. The screens in the hangar all began airing graphics for a Test of Might. Raven looked around the room to see the various Squires and Knights staring at the King.

"I hope you all have a wonderful day." The Drakon King said before walking out of the hangar. As he left the room, Raven felt the air move around him. Chatter had erupted amongst the room. Everyone was talking about the Test of Might. Everyone except for Crow.

"Raven, you don't know magic like I do." Crow said, "But you should have felt it there."

"Felt what?" Raven asked.

"The Drakon King stopped time. Completely. I don't know how he did it. It was a perfect stop. That would take immense magical power. I didn't realize it until he left the room." In six weeks spending every waking moment together, Crow never looked worried.

Before he could ask what was wrong, Raven felt a tap on his shoulder.

"So, are you going to say hi or what?" The voice behind him was Penguin.

"Hey Penguin." Raven said, "Congratulations on getting recognized by The Drakon King."

"Congratulations to you too." Penguin said, "The first person The Drakon King thought of, I'd be jealous if he didn't have better things to say about me."

"Very funny."

"Hey is he okay?" Penguin said, she looked over at Crow who was now muttering to himself.

"No. I am not okay. You're not either. We were just in a time warp. The Drakon King created a Time Warp as nonchalantly as you boil water on a stove. He's capable of magic on a scale that I never thought of. If you need me, I'll be in my room preparing until the Test of Might. I suggest the two of you do the same. The King didn't do us any favors. He put targets on our heads."

With that Crow left the room before most of the other Knights and Squires got over the shock and awe of seeing The Drakon King in person. Raven and Penguin looked at each other and silently agreed to do the same. They didn't know when the test would be, but they would be ready.

Chapter 12

In the two months that followed The Drakon King's announcement, Crow had doubled down on his training. He had come to the conclusion that while he was a natural and thus more talented than the average Squire, having practice at his own skills would make him better than the competition. When he explained this to Raven and Penguin, they laughed as if he'd just then discovered that fire was hot. He spent days at a time working on his Jiu Jitsu against his puppets.

After that he would practice various spells and summons. He made the decision that defensive spells weren't conducive to his own style as he couldn't maintain a defensive bubble while keeping a summoned creature in his dimension. After a while he developed a routine that satisfied his needs.

He would wake up every morning and immediately start a run on the treadmill. After an hour or so, he would practice his summoning and other magics. He could now perform small projectile spells in addition to his numerous summons and golems. Only then would he practice his Jiu Jitsu against a puppet which he implanted the memories of 10,000 high level championship matches. Crow never beat the puppet.

As Jiu Jitsu was a grappling only art, Crow dedicated an hour a day to his striking. The puppet he summoned in this case had 10,000 hours of Muay Thai and Kickboxing implanted into it. As with the Jiu Jitsu puppet, Crow never defeated the striking puppet.

He had done this nonstop with no rest days. There were very rarely breaks. Instead, Crow had become obsessed with the idea that the test was coming despite not being told when it would be.

On the sixty fifth day of his training, he heard a tap on his door.

"Open" Crow commanded the door as he climbed off the treadmill.

"Wow. I imagined your room to be less of a gym and more of a laboratory." Kiva said as she walked in the room. She was wearing a dark purple ship uniform which made her pink skin look brighter by comparison.

"Actually, it's both." Crow waved his hand and the room shifted to a lab setting complete with seven work tables. All of the tables except one were covered in parts of golems.

"A transformation spell." Kiva said, "impressive."

"Did you come here to talk about my lab or do you have something pertinent to tell me. I have a test coming up."

"You and three hundred other Knights of the Flock."

"So why are you here?"

"Call it boredom. Call it cabin fever. You were supposed to be protecting Mirai."

"Mission got called off. You're on the ship now so there's literally no reason to guard you."

"When's the last time you ate?" Mirai said her tone was between inquisitive and concerned.

"No idea." Crow answered honestly. His elven physiology made it so that he could go weeks without food.

"Slept?"

"I slept an hour last night."

"Took a day off training?"

"No time. I have to get ready for the test."

"You don't know when the test is." Kiva said in a serious tone.

"So." Crow responded

"So you're taking a shower, then you're taking break."

Crow didn't have a counter argument. Kiva took a seat in the lab while Crow showered and put on a pair of black shorts and a black sleeveless shirt. Kiva dragged him by the arm to the cafeteria. They sat in a booth and pressed the button to order the day's special, chicken parmigiana to their table.

"Eat." Kiva said sternly.

"I really do not want to."

"Well then Crow, if you don't eat. I will cast a spell on you to force you to eat."

"Wouldn't work. I place counter hexes on myself the entire time I'm running." Crow said plainly. He did elect to start eating, if only to appease Kiva.

"Who do you think is going to hex you?"

"I think that I will be hexed during the test." Crow said.

"Do you ever talk to anyone about this?"

"What?" Crow asked between forkfuls of pasta.

"Your anxiety." Kiva said in a concerned tone.

"I don't have anxiety."

"You definitely do."

"No I don't. It's impossible. Elves don't get illnesses."

"Aesopians live long lives just like Earth's elves and mental health is our biggest struggle. Besides that, you're half human which means you've got human weaknesses."

"Can we drop it?" Crow said.

"Fine." Kiva said, "but if you need to talk, I'm here."

The two ate in silence for a moment.

"So, what do you want to do now?" Kiva said as they finished eating.

"I'm going back to my room to train some more." Crow responded.

"So I guess I'm coming with you then." Kiva replied.

A few minutes later they were back in Crow's room which he had used magic to change into a battle field.

"So you just use magic to change your room into whatever you want."

"Yes and no. It's actually a pocket dimension. Each time I change it, any object that I forget about goes to an alternate version. But yeah. I've made a lot of alternate versions"

"So, why a battle field?"

"We're going to have a sparring round. You against me. Do you have your Golem?"

Kiva reached in her pocket and pulled out a small statue. She held it close to her chest and then dropped it on the ground. The statue vibrated and grew with each passing second. As it grew its details became clearer. This was a giant woman made of stone, mud, metal and other materials. The craftsmanship of the Golem was second to none. Its forearms and hands were much larger than its upper arms. Likewise, its calves and feet were similarly large. The rest of its body

45

continued to grow until it reached a height of about ten feet. At that size, Crow could see the small details. It had designs carved into its body that were filled with a bright blue stone of some sort. Its eyes were glowing pink gems of some sort.

"I made some improvements. What do you think?"

"Oh it's beautiful." Crow said.

"She. My Golem is a she."

"She's perfect." Crow said, "Does she have a name?"

"Pixie."

"So, are you fighting my Golem yourself?"

"Of course not."

Crow thought for a second as to what would be a good match up for Kiva's Pixie. A ten-foot Golem with arms and legs that size would have incredible defensive capabilities. He wasn't sure he had something designed specifically for that situation.

Crow waved his finger in a circle and a black portal opened between him and Kiva's Golem. A small man wearing a business suit with red skin, horns, and a tail walked out of the portal.

"You're gonna fight my Golem with that?"

"Watch who yer talkin' to toots. I'm a Demidemon straight outta Gehenna," The Demidemon said, "Crow. What can I do ya for?"

"Sparring match against the Golem." Crow said as he sat down with his legs crossed so that he could look the Demidemon in the eye.

"Alright let me think about this fer a second."

"It can talk?" Kiva said in a confused tone.

"You humans are all alike. Yes, I can talk. What part of Gehenna didn't you understand? Guh-hen-ahh. Hell. The underworld. The realm of the Beast. Land of the dead. The source of dark magic. I mean you might not know that. You're an Aesopian. Your magic comes from somewhere else. Crow though. He was born with own little plane of Gehenna all around him. Unfortunately, that came with me, Numcustos Bestia. Imagine that, I break free from Gehenna only to be bound to a new realm controlled by a Human..."

Crow waved his finger and Numcustos lost the ability to speak. If he didn't, The Demidemon would have talked until the day was over. It was a small spell that Numcustos Bestia was proficient at, forcing everyone in the area to have a conversation with him.

"He's putting on an act. Numcustos and I actually share our power."

Numcustos had been Crow's assistant as long as he could remember. When Crow discovered that he was constantly surrounded by a small realm of Gehenna, Numcustos was discovered shortly thereafter. Though Numcustos was very plainly cursed. He bore a magical tether to Crow and his realm of Gehenna. Numcustos could only be near Crow, his realm of Gehenna, or things Crow frequently touched.

Numcusto's primary role was care taker for all of Crow's creatures, minions, and golems. Outside of that, Numcustos did everything Crow needed from cooking to laundry when magic couldn't do it for them. On the occasions where Crow cooked dinner or did laundry, Numcustos would grow impatient or upset. In exchange, Numcustos only asked for Crow's protection from any larger demons that may come hunting him. No larger demons ever came hunting for Numcustos Bestia.

"Custo. I need you to go back in the locker and get me Madman."

The Demidemon nodded and walked back into the portal. A moment later it walked back out pulling a chain that was attached to the chest of a 9-foot tall, two headed Golem made of gigantic orange boulders. The Golem had white stripes painted on its chest and arms. This was Madman.

"You good, boss?" Numcustos said through a visible struggle.

"Stick around. If she beats Madman, you might need to fight yourself."

"Are you ready yet?" Kiva chimed in.

"Almost." Crow said back, "Madman, listen carefully. You are not to destroy this Golem, do you understand."

"Yes sir." Madman bellowed back.

"How do you get them to talk?" Kiva said.

"I'll show you when we're done."

Madman assumed a fighting stance and backed away from Pixie. Pixie backed away as well, her body language didn't indicate any sort of confrontation. Madman charged in swinging both arms. Jab. Cross. Jab. Cross. Double arm thrust.

Pixie lifted her gigantic arms to defend the punches. Every punch was stopped dead in its tracks. Jab. Cross. Jab. Cross. Jab. Jab. Cross. Hook.

Nothing so much as moved the Golem. Madman ran to try an attack from behind. Pixie twisted her gigantic stone torso so that she was no longer vulnerable. Uppercut. Cross. Jab to the body. Hook. Uppercut.

Still nothing. Crow looked over at Kiva whom was smiling as her Golem had taken little more than a scratch during this encounter. Striking wasn't going to work. Madman lowered his stance and tackled Pixie to the ground with a double leg takedown. The takedown was sloppy because Crow's own double leg was sloppy. It still got the job done. Madman moved to the mount position and began punching again. Hook. Hook. Hook. Hook. Hook. Hook.

Because of the position advantage Madman's punches landed more earnestly. They still had little effect.

"Madman use the beam cannon." Crow shouted. Madman wasn't a Golem he needed to issue orders to, but it was a fair warning for Kiva.

Madman opened its mouths as a bright yellow light flashed down onto Pixie, melting through her gigantic arms. A thud echoed across the battlefield that was Crow's room. Pixie had gone limp and dropped her arms to the floor. Madman stood up and began walking back to Crow when metal spear went through it's left head.

Crawling out of the fallen Pixie was a human sized metal, Golem. This one had shiny silver butterfly styled wings. It all made sense now. Crow and Madman has been fighting a shell.

"Allow me to introduce you to Pixie's attack mode."

Where Madman was incredibly fast by comparison to Pixie's shell, the attack mode may as well have been a mosquito zipping around a tortoise. Making matters worse, Pixie could now fly. Pixie landed a kick to Madman's stone stomach. Another to the back of his knees. A third landed in the space between Madman's heads.

Crow felt a small tug on the connection he had with Madman. Madman's left head no longer wanted Crow's guidance. Whether this was detected or completely incidental, Pixie chose that moment to sit on Madman's right head. Independent of Crow's command, Madman's gigantic stone fist swung and hit the right head and Pixie simultaneously causing the right head to spin around for a moment. Pixie was sent flying.

Now Madman's right arm was punching his left head and his left arm was punching his right head. Pixie flew back in for another attack. With Crow's last ounce of control, Madman pulled the spear out of his left head and used it to pin Pixie to the ground by her wing.

"Okay let's stop now." Crow shouted over to Kiva.

"Probably a good idea." Kiva replied. Pixie pulled the spear out of her wing and returned to the shell. Kiva walked over to the shell and placed a hand on its massive shoulder. The damage to Pixie was repaired.

Madman was still fighting itself.

"Numcustos!" Crow shouted.

"I'm right here boss."

Numcustos walked over to Madman. Madman swatted at the Demidemon but missed.

"Don't you dare. I'll take you apart and put you in the scrap heap."

Madman continued fighting amongst himself.

"Why are you even fighting?"

"He hit me." Both heads said simultaneously.

"Crow," Numcustos shouted, "are ya sure you want to keep this one?"

"Yes."

"Fine." Numcustos said. He reached into his suit jacket and pulled out the chain he had dragged Madman out with. Once the chain was secured, Madman stopped everything and stood up still.

"Thanks, Numcustos"

"Yeah yeah."

As the Demidemon walked away, Crow and Kiva laughed. Crow didn't realize but it was the first time he'd laughed in weeks. He wouldn't admit it, but he was glad that Kiva had decided to bother him that day.

"Are we training together tomorrow?" Crow asked.

"I'd like that. It'd be less boring here." Kiva replied with a slight smile on her face.

"Tomorrow, don't use Madman. He's on a serious time out." Numcustos yelled back to the pair.

"Fine. Maybe tomorrow we'll use a Beast instead of a Golem."

Chapter 13

"Let me get this straight, there's magic and there's Anti-Magic. Now you're saying there's a third one?" Raven said in a confused tone as he laid spread out on the grass in a simulation room.

"No." Penguin replied, "Wavelength is a type of Anti-Magic."

The two were in the midst of their fifth straight training day. For Raven it was always fun spending time with Penguin, no matter what they were doing. Training, by and large a necessary evil, was better with Penguin around.

"Before we keep talking," Penguin said, "are you done for the day?"

"I was done before we even started." Raven said as he reached over to his bag and pulled out a ration of food.

"I just realized." Penguin said, "where's your hat?"

"It got destroyed while I was on Aesop."

"Why didn't you just get another one?"

"I really can't. The hat was a relic from when they used slow speed rockets on Homeworld. Someone ordered it and it took 50 years to arrive. The company that made it probably doesn't exist anymore. I ordered it from a catalog of rescued rockets and had it customized. To get a new one there's a waitlist."

"Well then you deserved to lose it then. Jeez. Why would you take something so valuable to a mission" Penguin said in a scolding tone.

"Can we change the subject?"

"What now?"

"Where do you get Wavelength Anti-Magic?"

Penguin stood up and walked to a display monitor in the middle of the simulation room. She typed something that Raven couldn't see. Suddenly, the grass and sky began to fade. Raven felt himself begin to float as they were now in perfect map of the galaxy.

Raven never knew how to behave in three-dimensional float. Where Penguin was able to move around effortlessly, Raven felt the need to flail his limbs around in the environment.

"Dude." Penguin said, "You just stretch your arms in front of you to move forward. Behind you for backwards. Left for left. Right for right. It's not that hard."

Raven put his hands to his side and dropped straight down. After a second of panic he returned to flailing until he returned to his original position.

"Hands in front of you. Just like boxing. Think of it as training."

"I said I was done." Raven said.

"But I didn't say I was done." Penguin said before moving to another area of the map. Raven reached his hands toward her and followed. Penguin stopped in front of a world that looked like a white marble.

"What is this planet?" Raven asked.

"Planet Ali." Penguin replied.

"And why are we here?"

"We're here because this is where we're going to get Wavelength Anti-Magic."

"You never explained what it's supposed to do."

"It's an offensive Anti-Magic. You don't have any kind of way to take down a magic user."

"Okay. Why is the planet white?"

"Because it's cold."

"How cold?"

"You're not going to like it.

"What do you mean? I'm not going there."

Chapter 14

Raven was trudging through six inches of snow on Planet Ali. He was wearing thick boots and cold resistant clothes. Advancements in technology meant that he could wear a form fitting, Sub-Zero Suit under his clothing. Supposedly the suit was supposed to lack any sort of feeling. That was a brilliant marketing lie. At least the face cover he was wearing was heated and his goggles were fog proof.

"Remember when they said the suits weren't supposed to have feeling?" Raven said to Penguin whom seemed fine walking in the snow.

"Can you be an adult for the two days we're here?" Penguin said plainly.

"It'd be easier if I knew why we were here."

"We're here to get you Wavelength Anti-Magic."

They pushed along as the snow blew all around them. Raven may have hated it, but he knew that Penguin would never intentionally drag him on a quest for nothing. With the Test of Might coming, they would need any advantage that they could get.

Raven looked over his shoulder, the ship had disappeared from view. Still, there was nothing on the horizon. Cold, hopeless, snow blew all over. Looking forward there was no difference between the sky and the ground.

"We really should have run into something by now." Penguin finally said after they had been walking for a while.

"I am not happy." Raven said as he felt his toes start to go numb.

"Does it really matter? We're already here."

"Where is here?"

"Change your goggle settings to infrared."

Raven touched a small button behind his ear. Suddenly a large structure was visible in the distance. As they got closer to the structure it became apparent that it was being guarded by four armed bipeds. Each step they took closer, revealed more details. The creatures were covered from head to toe with fur that Raven could only see when he switched back to normal vision from infrared. The creatures had blue, ape-like faces with jagged protruding fangs creeping out from the lower halves of their mouths.

"Why did I let you talk me into this adventure?" Raven said.

"Because there's no way you would knowingly let me face off with these things alone."

Raven gripped the handle of his beam sword. He didn't activate it because the creatures didn't move. He glanced over at Penguin whom was holding a bow gun. She hadn't armed her weapon, instead she just held it.

Raven wished that he hadn't been talked into this "quick three-day quest" for Wavelength Anti-Magic. He didn't know that it was going to lead to an at least twelve on two standoff.

"Halt Knights." A booming voice said. The sound was louder than the howling wind.

"What do we do?" Raven asked Penguin.

"I said stop in the name of Lord Berg."

Suddenly something sliced through the air. Momentarily the snow stopped blowing. The air felt warm. Then just as suddenly, the air temperature dropped again. It was definitely an unnatural occurrence. That being said, it didn't feel magical.

Raven and Penguin halted.

"Do not rush into this." Penguin warned him.

A second wave cut through the air. Penguin fired a bolt from her bowgun. The bolt shattered in the air. It was at that point that Raven decided that charging in was the best strategy.

"I told you not to do that!" Penguin called back.

"Too late." Raven yelled back. He flicked the switch on his beam sword. Then sliced through a NRL's head just as it popped up from below the ground. In the twentieth century movies on Homeworld developed an entire genre called "zombies" based on NRL's. In the movies, the zombies always over ran Earth. This was propaganda. In reality, NRLs were infestations like roaches or rats.

Raven could tell the NRL had been hiding underground by an odd mound of snow.

The NRL's head rolled as Raven stopped and looked around for more. The large creatures erupted into a roar of approval as the Necromantic Reanimated Life-form laid headless on the ground.

Once they were certain that no more NRLs were in the area they approached the planet's native citizens.

"We thought you were preparing to attack us." One of the large creatures yelled out.

"No. We just needed the NRL to come out of hiding. Most NRLs are drawn to battle fields, it's easier for them to feed on fresh corpses than infect stronger warriors." Raven said as he put his sword away.

A few moments later, they were in a gigantic building that was definitely designed with the creatures in mind. The tables and counters were higher. This matched the chairs that each had extra support legs. Raven's feet were dangling over the edge of his chair as if he were a child. Everything was made of stone.

"Okay. I'm just going to come out and say it," Penguin said as soon as everyone was situated, "not one report I read said anything about any sort of NRL problem on this planet. I want your names and I want to know how a planet that is below the freezing point of a human body has NRLs."

"Names are such an Earth concept. We're all called Icicle. All of us. Our leader is an Icicle you named Lord Berg whom is not here. Our planet did contribute one Knight whom you named Albatross." One of the creatures said. It was the same voice as earlier.

"Interesting," Penguin said, "let's cut to the chase. We came here to learn about..."

"Wavelength Anti-Magic," the speaking Icicle said. He stood up from his chair and took a few steps toward Raven and Penguin, "all you Knights come here for the same business."

"So, is it really something we can learn to do?" Penguin asked.

"For you, no." Icicle said to Penguin.

"And why not?"

"You can access magic, nowhere near enough to call you a Mage, but I'm sure with time you can probably pull energy from another realm."

"I'm twenty-seven not seven. I've known that my whole life." Penguin replied. Anyone but Raven would have said her tone was anger, this was disappointment.

"I'm guessing that you probably have no Anti-Magic skills then."

"I never took the time to learn them."

"She can't learn them." Raven interjected. "Sometimes Anti-Magic charms react when she wears them."

"Well then." Icicle said as he turned his attention to Raven, "You can learn it."

"Great let's teach it to him." Penguin said, "Quickly we have to return to our ship within three days and our first is almost over."

"I cannot. Not until you pass a small test."

Raven was not excited at the prospect of taking a test while he was actively preparing for another test.

"Fair enough." Penguin said. She cast him a gaze that ordered him to agree. Raven for a brief moment questioned their friendship.

"Fine."

"Good. Usually, the test is a simple one designed to question your knowledge of magic and it's origins." Icicle said, "You do know the origins of magic, correct?"

"Magic comes from other dimensions that have universes overlapping ours. The running theory is that there are as many kinds of magical dimensions as there are planets in the universe. When someone casts a spell, they are actually using themselves as a conduit from a magical dimension to our own." Raven explained. He knew he was missing details.

"That's the basics. Anti-Magic is also energy from another dimension but it negates all the other magic types that I've seen at least. On Ali we have learned to weaponize it. Congratulations you would have passed the test."

"What am I doing instead?"

"You're doing what you do best as a Knight, protecting the people. We have a Necromancer somewhere in the area and now we have an NRL infestation because our mages can't practice spells in a place where Anti-Magic falls with the snow."

"You realize I'm just a Squire, right?"

"Tell you what. Your friend and anyone else you want can help you."

Chapter 15

Raven and Penguin were getting ready to go out and arrest the Necromancer. This was an all too common problem that communities had. Most Necromancers were just Mages trying to bring back a loved one from the dead. They would order a Necromancy Artifact and try a spell. The spell would backfire. Then there would be an infestation of NRL's attacking towns.

It was such a common scenario, they practiced role plays of it in the Knight Academy. Occasionally there were variants. An NRL might be recently deceased and attempt to return to normal life or a Necromancer would cast the spell to bring back a lost pet and continue with it for decades before discovery. None of it mattered. Necromancy was illegal.

The plan of attack was simple. Wait until dawn and follow the NRL's back to wherever they collected as a hive. Collect the Necromancer, then dispose of any NRL's they are unable to dispel.

"So, how's your boyfriend?" Raven asked Penguin as he tied his belt around his waist.

"Oh, we broke up a while ago. I have a new girlfriend." Penguin replied. She adjusted the settings on her weapons then reached over the table she was sitting at and grabbed an oversized travel mug."

"Good. I never liked him anyway." Raven said, "What's with the giant coffee."

"Puffin gave it to me when I started taking more dangerous missions. It has runes of protection carved on the inside."

"How's he doing?" Raven asked. He hadn't seen or heard from Puffin since before he left for Aesop.

"No idea." Penguin said, "Hummingbird let my family know that he was sent on a special mission a couple months ago and we haven't heard back since. Apparently, he's fine though."

Raven pulled his coat on and checked his pockets. He had everything he needed to clear out an NRL infestation.

"It's almost dawn." He said, "let's start tracking."

They set out to the frozen tundra. The blistering snow made tracking difficult save for the faint lines in the snow left by NRL's that had trudged through earlier. Raven and Penguin followed the trails until they disappeared. Once the trail went missing it was clear that an NRL was hiding in the snow and preparing to attack.

It became a game. Who could kill the most NRLs the quickest. Penguin killed the first one by shooting it in between the eyes with a flame imbued crossbow bolt. Raven took the second by stabbing an NRL through the eye. Their totals quickly reached double digits before they found themselves At the mouth of a cave.

Warm air blasted them as soon as they entered. Raven tapped a button on his goggles for a temperature reading, 55 degrees Fahrenheit. This was a stark difference to the -30 degrees that was just outside the cave. Penguin shot a bolt into the cave wall.

"What's that for?" Raven asked.

"When we need to leave, we have to make sure we come out the same way."

As they continued deeper into the cave, a faint orange light came into view. The deeper they went, the brighter the light. After thirty minutes or so the light was illuminating the entire area. The ground below them was littered in footprints and blood trails, a sign of heavy NRL activity.

"We're going to find the Necromancer soon. Can you do me a favor and not rush in?" Penguin said.

"I don't always rush in."

"I'm not arguing you. Stay back until I give the signal or I'll personally inform every Knight Commander how reckless you are before you even attempt the Test of Might, comprende?"

"Comprendo." Raven said dejectedly. He took a step behind Penguin but kept his blade at the ready.

The cave opened into a underground canyon. Raven and Penguin were on the top. To their left, a path started that wound its way to the bottom. The floor was lined with Necromantic runes. Looking over the edge there were hundreds, if not thousands, of NRLs. They were walking aimlessly about the path of the canyon. At the bottom there was a floating skeleton holding an orange glowing staff. Unlike the NRL's that were wearing torn clothes and in some cases rags. This skeleton was wearing a soldier's uniform. Resting upon its smooth white skull was an orange crown adorned with black jewels. The skeleton seemed to be speaking some sort of strange language that not even the Translation Mist understood.

Penguin signaled a retreat. The pair moved as quickly and a quietly as they could back to the opening of the cave.

"Penguin. Is that a Nought? Since when can Noughts fly?"

"Worse." Penguin said, "It's a Lich."

"A Nought is what happens when a person is overtaken by a magical artifact. They're just mindless instruments of destruction. A Lich is Necromancer being controlled by all the spirits of the dead they think they brought back. A Lich doesn't have just one mind, it has hundreds. It can think. It can plan. Most importantly, they can manipulate the dead they summoned unlike most necromancers. They're also immensely powerful."

"So what do we do?"

"We return to our ship and call for backup."

Before they could move, an NRL jumped on Raven's back and started choking him. Raven pulled down on the decaying arm that was across his throat, causing it to break. Penguin followed that up by shooting the NRL in the head, killing it.

"Penguin, am I gonna get suck and die now. The NRL definitely scratched me."

"No. Its a stupid thing in the movies."

The NRL on the ground that the Squires thought was dead began to let out a wail. Raven cut its head off and the wail continued. A thunder of footsteps could be heard from the cave. The NRLs had all ran out of cave, floating above them was the Lich.

Penguin fired a bolt at the Lich to no avail. The bolt just lodged in the Lich's exposed skull.

The pair tried running. Unfortunately they were being flanked. Dozens of NRLs were surrounding them on either side with hundreds behind them. Raven was sure there would be no escape.

Penguin fired a dozen bolts into the crowd, killing some of the NRLs. This was more an act of futility as more NRLs appeared.

"Surrender" The Lich wailed.

"Penguin it talks."

"I'm aware of that.

Raven reached in his coat pocket and pulled out an Anti-Magic talisman. It would buy them a few seconds to escape if he could dispel the source of magical energy. Now he just needed to place it on the Lich's staff.

An NRL jumped on Raven's back. The talisman activated. With a flash of white light, it was now just a stone coin. The NRL was a corpse on the ground. He didn't have anymore talismans.

A few NRL's jumped on Penguin and quickly recoiled as the effects of the protection wards she had cast on her took effect. She fired bolts into their skulls before they could get up.

The space the NRLs gave the Squires shrank. Raven estimated that soon he wouldn't have enough space to draw his blade let alone swing it. Oddly the NRLs weren't all attacking at once. It was as if the Lich was holding them back. This many NRLs could have trampled Raven and Penguin any time.

The Lich continued floating overhead.

"Surrender" The Lich wailed.

"No." Raven shouted back in defiance.

NRLs piled on top of Raven and Penguin. Raven turned his blade on and stabbed an NRL that was trying to bite his nose. The blade cut his chin as it slid into the NRL's chest.

"Surrender." Raven could heat the Lich clearer than he could hear his own thoughts.

Penguin must have had a taser of some sort on her person. A flash of light went off while several NRLs howled.

"Surrender." This time the wail was definitely inside Raven's mind. He wasn't sure if it was the Lich's voice or his own.

"No. I can't." Raven yelled back.

Suddenly, Raven was calm. His eyes closed involuntarily but he didn't panic.

After a few seconds he opened them again. He was now standing upright in what looked like an endless field with a blue sky. He bent over and picked a blue flower. He smelled it, it was a real as he could tell. Was he teleported? Did the NRL's knock him out and carry him through a magical gate? Was he dead? Under normal circumstances, these questions would have terrified Raven. Instead, he was tranquil.

"How is Earth your calming place?" A voice said, "Most humans have never even been there."

"Calming place?" Raven said.

"Yes a calming place. You are calm correct? This is all in your head." The voice said.

The Lich materialized along with a small table and two chairs. Instead of torn rags, it was wearing a clean black, Knights of the Flock uniform. The crown on its skull still resting, unmoved. Up close there was a crack in its skull where Penguin shot it with a bolt.

The Lich sat at the table and motioned for Raven to sit as well. Raven sat.

"Where are we?" Raven asked.

"This is the inside of your mind. I placed you under a calming spell so that we could talk." It struck Raven at that point that the Lich was no longer wailing. It had a normal speaking voice.

"Why do you want to talk?"

"I'm about to grant you access to everything I know about Anti-Magic including what you call Wavelength."

"Why?" Raven asked.

"You passed the test. The Drakon King and Lord Berg decided that there should be a test for someone to be able to deactivate the greatest weapon in history."

"So when did the test start?"

"I do not know." The Lich said, "Before you got to me. Most people that want to learn to deactivate Magic are Mages themselves. I can not pass this information to a Mage. Most people that want this information come alone. I can not pass this information to people without trusted friends. Lastly, most people when overwhelmed, give up. You have no chance as a Non Mage defeating over a thousand of my soldiers. Even with your friend."

"So what happens now?"

60

"Now you never need an Anti-Magic rune or talisman again. You can deactivate almost any spell from any distance."

"How?"

"You're going to want an object or two that you can channel this energy through. Otherwise it it'll be an explosion. A lot of Mages use spell books. Some use umbrellas. Wands were popular at various points in time."

"Would a sword work?" Raven said, thinking of his katana.

"What would you do if it breaks?"

"Good point."

"Think about it. In the mean time. Open your eyes."

Raven was again standing. This time he was back in the snow. To his surprise, The NRL's and the Lich were making their way back into the cave.

"So you passed?" An Icicle walked up from behind the pair of Squires.

"I did. I still don't know how to use it."

"That's the easy part. Think of something magical in your range and think about it stopping. The more you use the power, the greater the range will be."

"So who is going to explain everything that just happened?" Penguin said.

"I'll tell you everything on the way home."

"Before you go, you should try your Anti-Magic Wavelength on me." Icicle said.

Raven didn't know what was magical about Icicle but he thought about making it stop. A pulse of warm air erupted from his chest into Icicle. The pulse knocked Raven back in pain. He definitely needed a concentration object.

Icicle writhed on the ground. After a few seconds a tall, slender man wearing a floor length fur coat over a Sub Zero Suit stood up. The man stuck his hand out to shake.

"Congratulations Raven." The man said as he shook Raven's hand. Then he was gone. In his place on the ground, a dead mouse. Raven had never seen teleportation magic work. But he needed to collect the evidence. He reached down and picked up the dead mouse.

"Can we please go home now?" Raven said, "Everything about this planet is making my brain hurt."

Chapter 16

Crow was not amused. He was sitting at a table next to Kiva. Across from them was Raven, Penguin, and a stranger that wasn't a knight. The stranger was a normal human woman with shoulder length brunette hair, her name was Charly and she was apparently dating Penguin. At the head of the table was Mirai. They were playing some sort of game. Raven was the banker. Raven was an idiot.

"Isn't this fun guys?" Mirai said. She moved her piece around the board and collected money.

Kiva, Mirai, and Penguin were having fun. Crow was suffering. He didn't care what Raven or Charly thought. Perhaps it was because they could have spent that time training. Perhaps it was because they were in his room. Somehow, Kiva had convinced him that social interaction would be a good way to refresh himself for training. All Crow could think about was the upcoming Test of Might.

"Yes. So much yes." Raven said, "I'm glad you guys stayed on board the ship."

"Why did you stay on board Mirai?" Penguin asked as she rolled the dice.

"Nobility is allowed to watch the Test of Might." Mirai answered, "Some of the Knight Commanders even ask for our input in grading. So you better stop being a sour puss, Crow."

Crow was not amused. He rolled the dice and landed on a space controlled by Charly. She laughed as he gave her six of his cards. He could have used a token he'd earned earlier. But he wanted to be out of the game.

"Crow, I thought you had a friend coming."

"What are you talking about?"

A Gehenna door opened behind them. Crow didn't even need to turn around.

"Hey Crow, remember that Ice Nought you brought in a while back?" Numcustos Bestia said as he leapt out of the door and onto the table.

"I remember him." Raven said, "The shop keeper on Aesop."

"Do you want a cookie for remembering a near death experience big guy?" Numcustos said, "This must be that Raven mook you told me about."

"Numcustos Bestia, get to the point." Kiva said.

"Oh. My apologies," Numcustos said, "Yeah Timmy is pissed."

"Who is Timmy?" Crow asked.

"The Ice Nought."

"Why is he pissed?"

"Because I named him Timmy. He tried to freeze me."

"Is that all?"

"Hemlock and I used Timmy to make Iced Coffee."

"Hemlock?" Raven said.

"A Minotaur." Crow answered, "What else?"

"He's sharing an enclosure with a Fire Nought."

"Move his enclosure and stop using him for iced drinks."

"I don't have to change his name?"

"He has permanently changed to a monster; I legally could have exterminated him. He can be Timmy until he earns his keep."

Numcustos sprang off the table and back through the door. As he gleefully skipped out of view, the Demidemon could be heard yelling, "Timmy you're moving in with a Cerberus."

"Sorry about that." Crow said.

"Your pet ruined the game." Kiva said bluntly. Numcustos had knocked all the game pieces off the table during his scene.

"Sorry." Crow said, "I guess the game is over."

"It's not a problem." Mirai answered, "I knew that was going to happen."

The group laughed. Even Crow. Soon enough, Penguin and Charly left. Then Raven.

"So, Crow, are you ready for your test?" Mirai asked as she cleaned up game pieces.

"He's been ready for weeks. We just don't know when it will be." Kiva said.

"So this is the timeline where that's what's happening." Mirai said with a wide grin, "Oh it's in 4 weeks. You'll be notified tomorrow morning."

"Why didn't you tell me?" Crow replied. His anxiety over the test had dominated his thoughts over the past few weeks. Knowing when it was game him a sense of relief.

"And ruin a perfectly good game night!" Mirai yelled back, "Come along Kiva. The cafeteria serves late night desert on Wednesdays."

"It's Thursday." Crow and Kiva said in unison. Crow noticed that Kiva blushed slightly.

"It's Wednesday somewhere." Mirai shouted, "Come Kiva! We're off to get some delicious cakes… and gossip."

Kiva sighed as Mirai led her out of the room. As they left, Crow's phone vibrated in his pocket. The test was going to be in a month.

Chapter 17

"So, are you and Crow a thing now?" Raven asked Kiva bluntly. They were three weeks away from the test. Kiva had offered to help teach the Squire how to channel his Anti-Magic energy into an object for use. As Mages specializing in Golems, Kiva or Crow would have been the best people Raven could have asked. Crow immediately said no, citing Raven's "lack of learning ability."

"We're not, not a thing. But we're not a thing. I just like talking to him." Kiva replied. The answer didn't phase Raven so much as it would entertain Mirai whom had asked him to get the truth.

Raven reached his hand out and tried to push his new found Anti-Magic through his fingers into a coin. The coin wobbled on the table but nothing.

"Okay, why are you using a coin?" Kiva asked.

"It's something of value."

"Is it something of value, or something that you value."

"What's the difference?"

"One is an object that you're connected to, you care about. It's part of your story. The other is something you don't care about all that much."

Raven tore apart his bedroom looking for something that fit Kiva's description. He tried his lucky underwear to no avail. There was no reaction to his favorite water bottle. His video game controller yielded no result. A picture of his deceased father and sisters started to crumple and rip as Raven tried to embue it with his Anti-Magic. He instantly stopped. Even if he could print another one, he didn't want to destroy the original. Relics from The Resolution 1 were rare and precious.

"Can't I use my Anti-Magic without some sort of filter?"

Kiva reached in her jacket pocket and pulled out a cloth doll. She held it to her lips and whispered something. The cloth doll grew to roughly four feet tall. It had giant button eyes and zipper for a mouth. It looked as if it had been made in two minutes out of the remnants of a faded old blue t-shirt. It had one arm larger than the other.

"Deactivate this golem." Kiva said.

"That's a golem?" Raven asked.

"Yes." Kiva said, "Deactivate it."

Raven stretched his hand out. He concentrated to the point where he was sweating. Nothing. The patchwork golem did a dance. Raven tried again, nothing happened. The golem danced again. Raven sat down on the ground, crossed his legs, and closed his eyes.

"Just give up." The voice belonged to Crow whom had entered the room behind them.

"I'm not going to quit." Raven said, "I'm not sure what your problem is with me. But I didn't ask you to be here."

"You did." Crow said, "If you want magic to work for you, you need to require it to work."

Raven opened his eyes and stood up. Crow was standing next to Kiva whom was collecting her patchwork golem. Behind them, a giant door that definitely had not been part of Raven's decor prior to this.

Crow snapped his fingers and the door burst open. Hundreds of disembodied hands came flying out. They grasped Raven by every conceivable angle and pinned him to a wall. Two of the hands forced Raven's eyes open so he could see exactly what was coming toward him. A Minotaur was charging forward swinging a battle axe with it's horns angled in such a way that if the axe missed, Raven would be gored.

Raven broke into a cold sweat. He opened up to scream but a hand clasped itself to his mouth and muffled the sound.

"Stop this Crow!" Kiva shouted as the Minotaur's hoof crossed through the door and into their realm.

"No, if he wants to play Mage. We're going to make him learn the way I did. Now Raven, use your Anti-Magic Wavelength to send my Thousand Hands of the Needy and this Minotaur back through the door before they kill you."

66

Raven gasped for air as a hand on his throat began to squeeze. He wondered if Crow would actually kill him. He was certain he would pass out.

Before he faded, he felt a burst of warm air hit every pore on his skin. Suddenly he could breathe again as Crow's summoned beasts were sent back into the door. Raven dropped to his knees and coughed as he realized what had happened. He had used the Wavelength.

"What did it feel like?" Crow asked Raven while the latter was still on the ground.

"It felt warm." Raven choked out.

"Good remember that feeling. Now force it into something."

Raven finally caught his breath. He stood up and looked at Crow. He concentrated on the warm feeling he'd just had and forced it into a gold chain that his mother had given him before she died. It was much easier now that he knew what it was supposed to feel like.

"Thanks." Raven said. He meant it.

"Don't ask me for help again." Crow replied as he turned toward the door. "You're not an idiot; you should be able to figure this out without totems or gimmicks."

"Bye Raven." Kiva said.

Crow and Kiva left Raven alone in his room to clean up. It occurred to Raven that while he'd probably never be friends with Crow, there was a chance they'd be able to coexist in the future.

He attempted to use his Anti-Magic again but was unable.

Act 2: The Test of Might

Chapter 18

The day had finally arrived. The Test of Might. The day started like any other, Crow woke up before schedule, he summoned a puppet, and had a few quick sparring rounds. Numcustos Bestia prepared a breakfast for him. Crow chose not to question what the meat actually was.

"You know, if you leave the ship, you'll have to summon me like anyone else in your stable. Unless you move your home to wherever the test is." Numcustos said in a tone that sounded more like a warning than informing.

"I'm aware." Crow said.

"So, who all is going to take the test?"

"It doesn't matter; they aren't you. But if you must know, "Numcustos smiled, "Every last Squire."

"What's the test like?"

"How would I know?"

Crow cast a spell that silenced Numcustos Bestia and began to dress in his traditional suit of armor. Putting it on was a hassle. While it wasn't made of steel like the original Knights of the Flock wore, the armor was still very large. First he needed to put on the "chain mail." It was a thin layer of polymer material designed to mimic the look and purpose of actual chain mail, luckily, Crow's was bulletproof. Next came the greaves. The leg pieces slid on like regular pants but they were much denser. The greaves also limited his mobility as they weren't flexible. The boots were much the same.

Finally he slid the heavy top on. Armor now was graded for everything from a ballistic missile, to laser bolts, to a blast from a dragon. Not that Crow had ever worn it in battle.

The only Knights he ever saw wearing the traditional armor away from traditional events were either old, or Orcs. Older Knights were the reason that the traditional armor was still as prevalence as it was. The Drakon King himself was the one that changed the uniform rules to include the light armor and even civilian clothes if a Knight Commander allowed it.

Crow picked up his helmet and a supply bag. and marched toward the hangar for departure. The hallways of this corridor of the ship were flooded with his fellow Squires, each wearing their silver armor with the Squire's crest on their chest.

The hangar was as big a mess as the hallways. The area was flooded with Squires. Crow elected to stand in a corner by himself. Thankfully being shorter in a crowd meant that he was essentially invisible.

"Squires! Attention!" A voice said over the loud speaker.

The Squires lined up just as they had done at the academy hundreds of times. The Squire in front of Crow, an Orcman was carrying his boots rather than wearing them. Crow wondered if that level of embarrassment would be tolerated.

Standing on stage before the Squires were Knight Captains, behind them was one of the Royal Guard.

The first-person Crow could identify was Goose. Goose, a hulking Orcman that was even larger than some of the pure Orcs that Crow had met. Goose's armor was dented and scratched everywhere. Tied to his back was a massive iHammer, a weapon designed to bludgeon opponents to death while disabling any kind of technology they may have carried. His bright green skin, purple braided Mohawk, and white fangs had only added to his legend at the academy. When Crow was a child, he had a classroom visit from Goose whom described, in great detail, how he killed a giant sandworm and ate its heart on his first mission to Mars. Needless to say, Goose's Knight Squadron, the Gaggle were the most ferocious warriors the galaxy had seen.

To Goose's left was Hummingbird. She was a young, petite human woman, she couldn't have been older than 40. Her armor was immaculate. Her helmet and cape were adorned with colorful feathers that made her look friendlier than Goose. Hummingbird was known widely as the best teacher and leader among the Knight Commanders. It was she that appeared on all the advertisements recruiting new Knights to the Flock. In addition to managing her own squad,

Hummingbird was also the Knight Commander for all but a few Squires. She was very serious about the grammar in Crow's mission reports.

To Goose's right was Blue Jay. Blue Jay was an old elf. There was no way of knowing how old he was, he was the only old looking Elf that Crow could think of. He could have been 80, 800, or he could have been 8000 depending on what magical effects he was under. Blue Jay was valued for his ability to captain the pilots in the Knights of the Flock. Nobody in his squad had less flight experience than fifty years, which is to say his squad was entirely comprised of Elves and Dwarves whom had thousands of years to live.

Finally standing behind them with a long staff tied to his back was a tall thin elf. Every feature about him was beautiful from his chiseled jaw to his well-kept hair. The only thing that could have disrupted his perceived beauty was a scar that went from his eyebrow straight down his cheek. The elf was wearing a shimmering gold armor adorned with the crests of the Knights of the Flock and The Drakon King. This was Tempest, Crow's Father.

Crow was nonplussed at the sight of his father. He had learned more about The Drakon King's guard at the academy than he did in their few conversations. He was one of hundreds of children from dozens of wives. He didn't know how many siblings he'd had. He might even have a couple in the crowd with him. They shared DNA but they were not a family.

What Crow did know about Tempest was this, Tempest believed he was better than any living creature that he had encountered. He had spent lifetimes developing himself as a warrior and a scholar. The second American Civil War, World Wars 3 and 4, The Martian War, The Necromancer Rebellion, and The Andromeda Wars, all saw Tempest join the battlefield. Not coincidentally, Tempest was on the winning side.

Somehow Crow met eyes with Tempest and for a brief moment they shared a mutual feeling of disappointment.

"Squires." Blue Jay spoke in a hush tone into the loud speaker. "Those of you that wish to be pilots in the Armada may board the ship to my right. The rest of you will remain here for your test."

Only a couple dozen Squires left. As Crow predicted all but one were either an elf or a dwarf. The lone one, Verdin, was a human man that graduated with Crow. There was no way he would pass.

"Squires." Goose boomed into the loud speaker, "You have elected to take the honorable path. Some of you will be chosen for your leadership ability. Some of you will be chosen for strength. Some of you will be chosen for your willpower. But the majority of what I see here are Squires that will not pass, which means..."

"That you can try again next year." Hummingbird said as she pushed Goose away from the microphone. "This is a test based on reality. Your armor is set to test mode. Any injuries you sustain, including those that would normally be fatal will heal as long as you are wearing the armor in a testing environment. That doesn't mean that you won't feel it. You just won't die."

"That will be all, Knight Commanders." Tempest said, the Knight Commanders held three fingers over their hearts, the standard salute Knights gave to their superiors. Tempest walked to the microphone and started speaking.

"The Test of Might is to determine who is ready to be a Knight of the Flock. You can fail The Test and a Knight Commander could still want you for their squad. I could want you for the King's guard, of course that would mean you'd eventually have to change your code name. The Drakon King could elect to make you a Knight Commander. This will not likely be your last test but it could be your best test. From here on out, you are no longer on even footing with the people around you, some of you will emerge as superior."

The crowd buzzed with excitement. Though nobody spoke a word. Crow didn't think any of them were qualified for more than maybe a Knight. A low rank Knight at best.

"Your Test begins now. Behind you are three ships. If you're not on the ship at departure in 20 minutes. You fail."

A ship behind the Squires opened its bay doors and started its engine. Crow looked over and saw Raven turn and start running toward the ship. Penguin took off right behind him. Above them a monitor had a countdown that was down to sixteen minutes and counting.

Chaos erupted. Crow looked up at his father whom was smiling. The Orcman holding his boots got knocked out by some sort of spell. Crow was correct in his assumptions.

Crow wouldn't have the room to open a Gehenna Door amongst all these people. A Squire sucker punched him and made a break for the ship. Thought about retaliation but realized it was pointless.

This was not a test to determine who could get on the ship the fastest.

It was a test to determine who could make the right decision. The people that erupted into chaos at their first sight of adversity didn't deserve to be full-fledged Knights. Crow opened a door above him and summoned his Thousand Hands of the Needy. The skeletal hands formed a path over the heads of the Squires. He was gently lifted by two hands and walked into ship.

"Took ya long enough." Raven said to Crow as he boarded the ship. He wasn't sure why it made it him so frustrated. Raven had worked hard to-- achieve his goals. Still, Crow wasn't satisfied coming in second place to anyone, let alone Raven.

More people started piling into the ship. Each person was more beat up than the last. Crow, Raven, and Penguin sat next to each other in silence. Some of the Squires that were late to board the ship were still fighting. To Crow's surprise the Orcman without shoes was sitting across from him.

"Your spell, the Thousand Hands of the Needy. That's super impressive." The Orcman said as he scratched at his face.

"Do I know you?" Crow asked.

"I don't know. Probably." The Orcman said back.

"Why aren't you wearing your boots?"

"I prefer not wearing them whenever I can get away with it."

"And you thought the Test of Might was an appropriate time to not wear boots." Penguin interjected.

"I mean, I'm the one that made the test." The Orcman's skin changed from green to a dark golden brown. He sprouted a salt and pepper beard seemingly out of nowhere. His ears developed a point while his horns receded into his skull.

"Holy crap! It's The Drakon King." An onlooker said.

"Guilty as charged." The Drakon King said as he raised his hand.

All the Squires silenced.

"Why's everyone so quiet. I was just observing."

Nobody spoke.

"Oh. You all took that addressing nobility course. You have permission to speak freely."

Chatter erupted.

The Drakon King scratched his face. Everything stopped. Crow couldn't move but he could still see and hear.

"So, I keep having to stop your time. You have no idea how much energy it takes for me to stop whole areas and still keep you able to perceive things."

Crow tried to blink. He couldn't. Again, for a brief moment he was amazed at the amount of control The Drakon King had over time magic. He wondered if anyone else truly understood how insignificant they were compared to the king.

"By now you've probably wondered where we're going. We're going to Earth."

Suddenly Crow was able to move again. He along with the group were stunned. Homeworld, Earth. The richest, most powerful planet in the known universe. Home to the humans. Home to the elves, dwarves and orcs. The cross point of all magic.

The Squires hadn't departed and the test was beyond all of their wildest expectations.

"By the way. Nobody here has failed yet. So, you can all be relieved. Once we land, we're going to show you to your rooms. After that, tomorrow you're going to have the second part of the test."

"What's the second part of the test?" a Squire said, breaking The Drakon King's monologue.

The Drakon King smiled. Up close his features seemed almost godlike. The smile somehow calmed his nerves. Crow stared directly into The Drakon King's eyes wishing for a moment that he could understand everything The Drakon King could about magic. The Drakon King exuded an air of confidence and power.

"The next stage of the test will be an old-fashioned joust." The Drakon King said, "We are going to go over the specifics at dinner."

Chapter 19

The first thing Raven noticed at the dinner was that Crow looked nothing like his father. For that matter, Crow barely resembled an elf other than his height, even then Crow was notably shorter than the average elf. Where Tempest had sharp features and gold skin, Crow's skin was dark brown with almost a gray tint. Tempest had perfectly maintained hair and nails; Crow's hair was in messy dreads on the top of his head. The crests beneath their left eyes were even different shapes and shades of blue.

They were in a gigantic ball room. Most of the tables were filled with Squires. Though a few tables had Knights and Knight Commanders and other ranking officials stationed with them. Every Knight and Squire was wearing their traditional armor. The walls were adorned with hanging artwork depicting the landscapes of several planets.

At Raven's table was Penguin to his left. To his right was Owl. Owl was a very close friend of Raven of and Penguin that had been stationed in distant missions. Of the three of them, Owl had been the fastest to graduate the academy. It was a relief to see her at the Test of Might. Owl was slightly taller than Penguin with a thin but muscular frame from years of running for fun. Her armor had a golden cross on the right shoulder, signifying that she was a medical specialist.

Across from Raven was Condor. Condor was a more experienced Squire that Raven had done a few missions with. They had common interests but hadn't socialized before this. Condor had the classic dwarf look. He had a beard superior to any human. He was short and stocky. What betrayed Condor's appearance as a classic dwarf was a Mage's crest under his left eye. As far as

Raven knew, there had never been a Dwarven Mage before.

Next to Condor was Swan. Swan was a captain in The Gaggle, Goose's squad. Swan was known as "The Glamrock Vampire Princess." Her vampirism was unconfirmed, though most likely was a moniker based around her personal style and flair for the dramatic. She was the first woman that Goose had ever recruited. Swan was known far and wide as an agent of positive change. She advocated for education for all, defended the rights of all species and genders across various planets and was an accomplished writer. Raven had read several of her books and was excited that she was at their table.

Before he even spoke, Penguin elbowed him in the ribs and whispered, "I know Swan is here but you don't get to ask her every question that pops in your head."

Closer to front of the room was The Drakon King and a few of his own personal guests. Mirai was among them, wearing a purple gown that had a high collar.

Raven scanned the room for Kiva. Unsurprisingly he found her at Crow's table. She was also wearing a high collared gown. The other two people at their table were Squires that Raven did not know.

"So, what inspired Mist at Midnight?" Condor asked Swan to Raven's excitement.

"It's all a metaphor for my first time on a mission away from my ship. I was just so excited to be out and helping people, I had to write about it."

"Who's leading the kill count?" Raven asked. The kill count was an illustration of the brutality the Gaggle was known for. They published their kill count quarterly. The winner at the end of the year was given a vacation. At the academy, Raven read the Kill Count more religiously than he read some textbooks.

"I am. Followed by Goose. Followed by Mallard. Though you know Kill count is just a name. It really counts any battlefield removal. Injury, retreat, mind control, surrender… and in the case of some particularly stubborn insurgents, death." Swan answered calmly, "But we're not here for me. Tell me who are you all. Off the battlefield if possible. I've read all your battle records."

"I'm a nerd." Condor said with a smile on his face, "I have a wife and two sons."

"I spend a lot of time reading and meditating." Raven said, "Penguin and I have game night every week."

"I really don't know what I want to do." Penguin said, "I've always just taken charge of situations I find myself in."

The main course was brought to each table. Magic must have been involved because each person's main course was different. Raven's was a very artistic display of mozzarella sticks around an entire fried fish on top of a bed of ravioli. Penguin's was an old family recipe, arroz con grandules accompanied by several pork dishes. Swan had a vegetarian dish, while Condor had meatballs roughly the size of baseballs. Each dish was aesthetically pleasing to say the least. Around the room some people had their food shaped into sculptures. Some people had their food come out on fire. Others even came on floating plates.

The Drakon King stood up at the front of the room.

"Are you all enjoying the food?"

"Yes sir!" The squires all said in unison.

"There is no stage. There is no microphone here. I'm not eating in front of you. I'm eating with you. The reason we're eating together is that everyone in this room has taken the step you're all about to take. Some of us a little longer ago than we'd care to remember... or admit" The Drakon King started.

The crowd laughed. Except Blue Jay whom was acting as if he hadn't heard The Drakon King's age remark.

"Tomorrow," The Drakon King continued, "You will compete in the first event of your Test of Might. It will be a Joust. You can of course build your own steed if you're a mechanical expert or utilize Golems or any other spell to bring a steed here to Earth."

Raven frowned. He had neither technical talents nor magical abilities. Several other Squires looked dejected as well.

"If you don't have one. You will be given a Horse from my personal stable. Don't worry they are magically fortified and specifically bred for such activities." The Drakon King added. A collective sigh of relief could be heard.

"Last thing. Budgerigar and Pardalote. You failed. There's no way I'm letting people get drunk during the most important test in their lives and think they wouldn't do that on a mission."

Two Squires were escorted from the dining hall. Reality set back in. They were in a test. Everyone of the Squires' careers were on the line. Raven finished his meal without speaking another word. Nobody spoke.

After dinner they were escorted to their individual rooms. Like dinner, the rooms were customized to the Squires. At least, that was Raven's assumption. He couldn't imagine that everyone wanted to sleep in a hologram of an open plain. Unlike the holograms on the ship, this area felt real. It had smells and sounds. There was a wild animal off that Raven couldn't identify in the distance.

Raven laid down and stared up the stars. He closed his eyes and imagined the next day's challenge. Beyond being incredibly difficult, a joust would be fun. The test did not intimidate Raven.

Chapter 20

Crow woke up in a laboratory littered with Golem parts. If there was a bed, he didn't use it. All he needed was the floor. The floor and water. The floor, water, and an alarm clock that was now screaming at him to wake up and put on his armor. For some reason, as he thought used magic to bathe, dress himself, and even brush his teeth; he thought back to his teachers at the academy.

"Crow, you'll never get far if you use magic for everything." They would say. Obviously, they didn't call him Crow but as a Knight of the Flock, he couldn't remember his birth name. It was likely a side effect of the ritual of becoming a Knight. Any time he tried to remember his name, "Crow" was all he could remember. Not that his name mattered. Even after becoming a Squire, he had been referred to as "Crow, Son of Tempest," by most people on the ship that knew his relation.

Crow stopped thinking about his past life and instead concentrated on the task at hand. He waved his hand and several small doors opened beneath the projects he had built the previous evening.

There was no scheduled breakfast or lunch for the Squires that day. There was a buffet that they were open to eat that morning but as Crow passed, it had hardly been touched. The Hallways of the King's Palace were ludicrous in size, much like the palace itself. Supposedly a group of Giants could walk through the halls with no issues. Even Orcs seemed small in the hallway. Not that Crow believed any Giant had ever walked the halls.

"Spent all night building something didn't you?" The voice behind Crow was Kiva.

"Are you following me?"

"No. I'm getting breakfast with Mirai. I just wanted to tell you good luck today."

"Thanks." Crow said.

A short while later Crow was sitting in a locker room with several of the Squires. A small robot was whizzing about the room handing all of the Squires their assignments for the jousting competition. Crow would be jousting Loon.

Loon was three years older than Crow. He was infamous for carving off an opponent's ear during a training exercise while at the academy. From that point on, anytime someone used excessive force it was called, "pulling a loon."

Only two Squires sitting in the locker room were completely separated from everyone else. Crow and Loon. Loon was doing a handstand against a wall on the other side. He was a thin human man with blonde, shoulder length hair. Even upside down he had a piercing quality about his blue eyes.

Crow saw several Squires finding their opponents and shaking hands. Crow wasn't interested in sportsmanship. Loon looked at him and held up a less than friendly hand gesture. It was a relief. Crow wasn't looking for a new friend.

Crow made his way to the stable ahead of his matchup. A porcelain shelled, human shaped robot greeted him with a friendly wave.

"Squire Crow. Will you be utilizing our mount options for your Joust today?" The robot said in a friendly tone.

"No." Crow replied, "I can summon my mount."

"You have four minutes and thirty-two seconds before your Joust. Please prepare your mount in Stable B."

Crow made his way to Stable B through the growing crowd of competitors. As he began setting up his summoning spell, he looked up to see Loon seated atop a mechanical rhinoceros. This must have been some sort of rule violation.

"Excuse me." Crow shouted over to Loon, "Is that allowed."

"It better be." Loon said as he cast a menacing gaze toward Crow.

Crow summoned Numcustos Bestia.

"Crow. What cha need already?"

"I've have two minutes. Get me the Gehenna Beast."

"No."

"I command you to go get me the Gehenna Beast."

"He's asleep. I can get you your Horse Golem. You know the one you literally spent last night working on."

82

"Look at that." Crow said, motioning toward Loon's Mount.

"Is that allowed?"

"Yes."

"Fine. I'll go get him. If he bites me again, you better heal me."

Numcustos opened a small door to Crow's realm of Gehenna and closed it behind him. Seconds later a much larger door opened. What emerged looked like a gigantic feline-esque creature with long grey and blue fur that followed no pattern in particular. It had long whiskers that touched the ground. Each of its paws were overshadowed by gigantic claws that were longer than Crow's fingers. Its head was crowned with two devilish horns.

Every labored breath the Gehenna Beast took, it exhaled smoke that smelled like the feeling of failure. Crow was sure to avoid the beast's mouth, lest he fall into a sense of existential despair that could potentially end in the Gehenna Beast feasting on his spinal fluid.

"Whatever you do, don't let it near an any sources of public water. We tried to toilet train it a couple months ago."

"Did it work?"

"It wasn't a question of could I." Numcustos said, "It was a question of should I. Did you know, Gehenna Beasts piss acid?"

"No."

"Neither did I!" Numcustos shouted.

"Why would I need to know that?"

"You don't. Just know I'm glad you never summon anything aquatic. They are still pissed at me. Also, I promised Justice the Gehenna Beast that you'd feed it."

Crow frowned.

"Don't worry he'll eat any bones. Especially if you can find a fresh spine."

The Gehenna Beast hissed.

"I'm sorry." Numcustos Bestia said, "Not chipmunk bones, they give him indigestion."

Crow resolved to feed the Gehenna Beast after he defeated Loon.

Chapter 21

Loon was legendary amongst the Squires. Five years before Crow graduated the academy, Loon's father, a teacher, was arrested in the middle of the school day. Crow wouldn't learn until later that it was because Loon's father was part of a conspiracy to steal a ship and fly to a distant planet. Loon's father was never heard from again.

Legend had it that the day Loon's father was arrested was the day that his mother began her quick descent to madness. As a child Loon would spend his days cleaning his home. His evenings he would spend hiding from his mother. At night he would teach himself to utilize his Magic talents.

There was a rumor that when Loon was eight years old, he was found torturing small animals and insects. As Crow heard it, Loon explained to his therapist that the way he treated his pets the way his mother treated him. He never went back to the therapist and came to school the next day with cuts on his legs.

Of course, everyone knew about Loon's incident at age 17. During a sparring match with another Squire, Loon used a pocket knife to carve off his opponent's ear. When his opponent didn't surrender despite missing an ear, Loon reached in to pluck their eye out. The teacher was forced to intervene. Luckily magical healing could reattach a missing eye and ear. Still, the fact that he was willing to dismember a classmate for what was ultimately a small class project was a highlight to the cruelty that Loon was capable of.

This cruelty was readily apparent to Crow as he swerved out of the way of Loon's lance. Rather than aim for the chest, the easier target, Loon aimed the top of the lance toward Crow's head. Crow ducked as best he could on the back of his Gehenna Beast.

They were in the midst of their Joust. Neither opponent had scored a point by knocking the other off of their mount while charging at each other. The first to two points would be the victor. Viewing them was a crowd of Nobles, Knights, The Knight Commanders, and The Drakon King.

Crow charged forward. He landed a clean blow but was unable to knock Loon off of his mechanical rhinoceros. At the same time, Loon drove his lance into Crow's shoulder. Crow felt a slight pop as the force from the blow knocked his shoulder of place. He wiggled his fingers to see if anything was broken, it luckily wasn't. Still holding the lance was suddenly exhausting work.

They charged each other again. Crow hit Loon directly in the chest. Loon slid backwards a bit but caught himself before falling. Loon's lance aimed for the stomach and drove the wind out of Crow. Gasping for air the next strike knocked him down onto the mud. He looked up and for the first time realized just how many people were watching him. He cast a quick spell to remove the dirt and mud from him and hopped back on the Gehenna Beast.

The Gehenna Beast charged without Crow's provocation. This time it jumped over Loon's lance. This was why Crow picked the Gehenna Beast instead of a Golem, it could think to itself. On the next charge, the Gehenna Beast shot a fireball at Loon's mount causing a brief moment of chaos. Crow capitalized by knocking Loon off of his mount.

Now tied at one point a piece, Loon charged forward even faster than before with a crazed look in his eye while the tip of his lance was directed at Crow's throat. In return, Crow charged with his lance set to collide with Loon's chest. Both lances broke.

Both riders returned to their stables and emerged with new lances. For some reason, Loon was emerging slowly. His rhinoceros had reached the defined limit of its fuel. Loon had the machine plod forward but after a few steps it stopped completely.

This was Crow's opportunity. He charged forward as quickly as the Gehenna Beast would allow him to. With one final strike, Loon crashed down into the mud.

"This contest is now over!" The voice over the loudspeaker did not sound familiar. There were cheers coming from the audience. The Drakon King and Knight Commanders had emerged from one of the stadium entrance tunnels.

Crow and Loon kneeled immediately.

"Bravo Crow!" The Drakon King said, "Bravo indeed!"

The Squires rose.

"So now, we come to my favorite part of the game. Knight Commanders, what shall happen to the winner?"

"Your Majesty, we have decided that we need to see more of this one to decide where he would best fit. Crow would perform well in all three of our squads, but he is by all means a once in a generation talent. We want to put him where he belongs most. So, we decided Crow will continue." Hummingbird said with such poise and grace, that Crow could never imagine her jousting in the mud.

"Understood. Crow, you have the honor of the next portion of the test."

Crow nodded his head.

"What of the loser?" The Drakon King asked, "What have you decided with him?"

"We do not need to see more of Loon." Goose said in a deep baritone that was characteristic of Orcs, "He is unruly. He lacks honor in combat. He was not trying to win the game; he was trying to injure Crow. Based on his performance today, it was clear that he would never fit anywhere else than my squad, The Gaggle."

"I'm not surprised to hear you say that at all." The Drakon King says.

Crow was surprised. How had Loon been given a spot on a Knight Squad but not Crow. He frowned slightly.

"Crow." The Drakon King said, "Do you accept your fate?"

"Yes, your majesty." Crow said. He didn't know what to think, both combatants had passed, but only the winner needed to continue the test. Even a year ago, he would have been infuriated.

The Drakon King spoke again, "Loon, do you accept your fate?"

"Yes, your majesty." Loon replied with a wide unhinged grin splattered across his face.

The Drakon King and the Knight Commanders disappeared and reappeared in their skybox. Crow concluded that The Drakon King must have stopped time to discuss the test results with Hummingbird and Goose at the end of every joust.

Crow walked back into his stable as Raven emerged for his Joust on a large, black, horse.

"Good job, Crow." Raven said. Crow could hear the smile on his face.

"Apparently not good enough."

"Loon's super tough. I don't know if I could have beat him." Raven said.

"Just don't lose this one." Crow replied.

For a fleeting moment, Crow felt like he and Raven were almost friends. Then the moment passed. Raven was a nobody. Raven would only hold Crow back. Raven was untalented. Yet there was something intangible about Raven that Crow was somewhat jealous of. It wasn't that he hated Raven, not anymore. He just wasn't ready to be friends.

Chapter 22

Jousting was much easier for Raven than it was for Crow. He was thankful that he hadn't drawn Penguin, or Owl, or Condor. Instead, he drew Turtledove. A large part of the difference in their matches was the fact that Turtledove, was under no control of her horse most likely due to fear.

At one point, Turtledove was the object of Raven's admiration, though he had never once acted on it, or even admitted it to someone that wasn't Penguin or Owl. She was a human woman with long dark hair and olive skin. Her eyes were a shade of yellow that made them resemble gemstones. Turtledove was a mage, though she often put makeup over her seal to make her face more symmetrical. She was the second youngest daughter of Saturn's regent though her humility never betrayed that fact.

Raven and Turtledove were both considered the "failures" of their Squire Class with Raven only having one fewer successful mission than Turtledove. As a result, they both spent hours per week doing additional training. Where Raven saw steady improvement in his abilities, Turtledove saw none.

Overtime rumors began to surface that Turtledove had changed her attitude. She stopped being herself in training sessions. She began refusing to partner with Squires that had lower success rates. She developed a penchant for obeying the rules and giving orders. She also stopped smiling.

Eventually Turtledove was able to string together successful missions. Raven once took the time to congratulate Turtledove on her new found success with a text message. Turtledove responded with a three-word response, "We aren't friends."

The first point came easy. They charged full speed at each other. Before they could meet and try to knock each other down, Turtledove's horse threw her off it's back. Turtledove climbed back up, covered in mud. Neither combatant was sure if that counted against her score. It broke Raven's concentration when he heard a judge call out, "one to zero, Raven."

They charged each other again. This time, Raven and Turtledove were able to make contact. Turtledove was able to hold on after being struck with the lance but was nearly thrown off again.

"Hey Turtledove," Raven shouted, "It's obvious that the horse you're on is not friendly enough for you to ride it. Do you want to ask if we can get you a new horse and start over?"

"No!" Turtledove said defiantly, her voice could only be described by Raven as adorable.

Raven felt himself sinking into the ground. His horse began to panic. Though it couldn't seem to move. Instead, it made loud, pained noises. She must have cast a spell to stop Raven's horse from moving. Raven tried using a Wavelength to disable the spell to no avail. He still could not use his new ability on command.

Turtledove charged full speed toward Raven as he briefly closed his eyes and braced for impact from her lance. When he was hit it felt like a cannonball hitting him in the chest. Knocking Raven off of his horse, face first into the mud. Raven began formulating strategies for scoring the winning point on the back of a horse that was unable to move. Surprisingly, the next thing he heard was the horn to signal the end of the Joust.

It wasn't the lance that connected. Turtledove was thrown from her horse into Raven which had incidentally knocked him off his horse. Lying next to him in the mud was Turtledove. She was a classic elf, pointed ears, larger eyes, and a slender frame that even the armor couldn't make appear larger. Raven stood up first and reached down to help her up.

"You almost had me there." Raven said as Turtledove stood up.

"Don't lie." She replied.

"What are you talking about?"

"You could have finished me off at any point." Turtledove said, "You have everyone convinced that you're some dumb oaf that rushes into battle without thinking. But I'm not fooled."

"What makes you say that?"

"I can tell when someone has Anti-Magic. My spell should have frozen your legs and your horse completely. I'm willing to bet you probably channeled it into your boots. That's why you can stand up now. If you wanted to be free, you could have kicked your horse."

Raven was shocked that Turtledove had figured out his entire plan. The only detail she was missing was the fact that he tried to emit a Wavelength when faced with the spell.

"Absolutely wonderful, Raven," The Drakon King and the Knight Commanders appeared from seemingly nowhere, "Knight Commanders what say you of the victor?"

"We've had nearly endless discussion on Raven, sire." Hummingbird said, "I found his mercy to be refreshing though it stifled what could have been a dominant performance. Blue Jay is right to believe he has a level of talent that this Joust was just not enough to display. Goose is of the mindset that he was merely playing with his food. Though we are all concerned about his record in missions and his reputation toward impulsiveness. It doesn't help matters that he didn't win this contest, Turtledove lost."

"So, what have you decided?" The Drakon King asked.

Hummingbird said with a smile, "We have decided that he continue on in the test."

"Very good." The Drakon King said.

"And Raven," Hummingbird said in an almost teasing tone.

Raven gulped, "Yes ma'am."

"Please show off that Anti-Magic, I didn't approve your little trip for it to go unused."

"Yes ma'am." Raven said.

He rushed off before hearing Turtledove's decision so that he could watch Condor, Penguin, and Owl's matches at the other field. He arrived just in time to see Condor win aboard a gigantic mechanical spider. Raven couldn't see whom Condor defeated but it was a fairly impressive showing. Condor didn't use his lance or even charge, instead he used the spider's legs to push his opponent off their horse as they approached. When Condor won, Raven cheered louder than anyone in the stands. Condor was chosen to continue on in the test.

Next was Owl. Owl utilized enhancement magic to make her horse faster and more durable. This was a long affair of running up and down the field until eventually her opponent began to tire. Eventually her opponent's horse fell and refused to stand.

"Well, I've never seen someone use fatigue as a weapon."

Raven looked up to see Tempest. Up close he seemed like a tall, frightening version of his son, Crow.

"It's kind of her specialty. Enhancement magic is what she uses to aid in her medical studies as well. This could take a while."

"It's funny, sometimes all you need to win is to outlast your opponent."

"I guess it kinda is." Raven replied.

Tempest walked away as it was decided that Owl would be moving on to the next stage of the test.

Penguin had a wrist mounted crossbow that she fired at her opponent as soon as the Joust started. Holding her lance with one hand she was able to knock her opponent out cold before her horse moved a single step forward. It was against the spirit of a joust but it was a win nonetheless. Penguin too moved to the next round.

Chapter 23

Puffin was in a hospital bed. He didn't know if he was on a planet or in a ship. But he knew that he was in a hospital bed. He knew that his limbs had been magically reattached. He could feel the slight tingle at his joints where magical threads were now holding him together. As a boy, he'd lost a finger to a sandwich. His father, a rune specialist reattached his finger several times.

Beyond that, he knew that someone had attacked him. Most importantly, he had figured out why.

"Puffin, are you awake?" The voice was Hummingbird. Perhaps it was the drugs he was on, but she seemed more like a spokesmodel than ever. He felt instant guilt. Hummingbird was his Commander; she was well beyond him in every status that he could imagine.

Puffin opened his eyes. He was glad that he didn't vocalize any of his thoughts. Surrounding him were Hummingbird, Goose, The Drakon King and the Royal Guard. For all of those ranked officers to be in one place, Puffin needed to be on Earth. More so, he must have been in The Drakon King's Compound. How long had he been asleep. It was at least a few weeks based on the field outside his window. He was attacked during Earth's winter; it was now spring or summer.

"Puffin." Hummingbird said.

"Yes Commander." Puffin said.

"Before we begin. How are you feeling?"

"I'm concerned because I was completely dismembered. I'm afraid my left and right pinky toes may have been switched when they were reattached. I feel like I let my kingdom down. I also feel a slight attraction to Hummingbird but I would never act on it as she is my superior officer."

Puffin stopped talking. He felt his face redden.

"I'm sorry Puffin." Hummingbird said through a slight smile. "I should have told you that you were under an honesty spell."

"I'm not sorry." Goose said, "Now I can ask you what you want without resorting to my usual tactics."

"I'm glad. I had nightmares about you every night as a child." Puffin said out loud despite trying not to with every fiber of his being. The spell wasn't just compelling him to tell the truth; it made him say any truth he may have experienced.

"It is imperative that you tell us who or what attacked you." The Drakon King said. His tone was far more serious than he normally presented.

"It was a Beast Knight." Puffin was not sure how he knew that.

"Beast Knight?" Goose said, "What in Gehenna is a Beast Knight."

"I do not know, Sir." Puffin said honestly.

"He doesn't know, how doesn't he know?" Tempest said. It was at that moment that Puffin realized that Tempest was the only one of the three Royal Guards that actually spoke. He wondered if that was always the case or just for occasions in public. He had read hundreds of reports where quotes were attributed to Easter and Tornado, yet here they were, the essence of silence.

"I don't understand. If you experienced a person, you should know everything about them."

"I didn't experience a person. I experienced a Beast Knight."

Chapter 24

Crow politely cut his egg in half before adding salt to it and taking a conservative bite. He took care to create no mess. With his family freely walking around the castle, he could not afford to create a scene. By his own admission, he may have been taking too much care, but he had seen at least two of his brothers punished for making their family look less than regal.

"So, you're the one raised on the ship. The Reclamation, was it?" Seated across from Crow was a an elf noble. The elf was tall and thin, like their father though he shared none of the same facial features. This one looked wild with wide, green eyes. He had black hair that stood out on end as if he'd been electrically shocked. He was wearing a three-piece suit. Crow didn't know most of his siblings but this definitely was one.

"The Resolution." Crow replied.

Crow's brother frowned, "How old are you anyway?"

"Does it matter? I'll look like this for hundreds of years."

"Would you take that tone with father?" His brother sneered.

"Would you like father to know that you're using his name as a threat."

"How old are you?"

"If you must know, I'm twenty seven." Crow said.

"My goodness." His brother laughed, "I've had more than ten of your lifetimes. Aren't you just adorable."

"One of us is a Knight, Renrassic." Crow said, "leave me alone."

"Brother, or should I say, halfling. I've spilled more blood than you can imagine."

"What do you mean halfling?"

"Halfling. Half human. Less than elf. What was your mother? Some sort of concubine for father. Do you know what Elves used Humans for in the Iron Age? They were pets. We'd breed them, feed them, use them for our pleasure and in the blink of an eye, they would be dead. Is that what your mother was Crow? Did father make a mistake with a spoiled bitch and make you"

As Crow prepared to trap Renrassic in his private dimension and feed him to the Gehenna Beast, a large hand tapped his shoulder from behind.

"Hey Crow, why don't you come eat with us. It might be worth going over strategy."

Crow didn't feel the smile form across his face, but there it was. He was relieved that he could escape a dreadful conversation for which he foresaw no exit.

"I think I shall take my leave to sit with the Squires." Crow said to his brother, "speaking with you was just as pleasurable as always."

"Likewise," Renrassic said with a smile.

"Oh, and you, Renrassic," Raven said before walking away, "I'm not sure about elves or nobility, but in human culture, I know more than one person has been killed for insulting another man's mother."

"I don't believe I asked you, peasant." Renrassic replied.

"I was just offering some advice."

Crow and Raven walked over to a table with Condor and Owl. Surprisingly, he almost instantly felt like sitting with his brother would have been preferable. If they had been talking before Crow sat down, nobody said a word once he and Raven appeared.

"What kind of strategy did you want to discuss?" Crow said in an attempt to break the silence.

"We wanted to go over..." Raven started to say.

"No Raven. Before we start sharing with Crow I have something to say," Penguin said. She was glaring at Crow as if she could melt him with her vision.

"What could you possibly have to say to me, we barely even talk."

"Exactly. Do you even know how to be nice to other people. I just watched it happen. Your brother was tearing into you so Raven decided to go save you and you don't even have the nerve to thank him. You act all high and mighty but you were last to get on the ship here. You damn near lost your joust. On top of that you're so nervous around your family I almost pity you." Penguin said.

"Almost."

"That's enough Penguin." Raven interjected.

"No he needs to hear this." Penguin said to Raven before turning back to Crow, "I have watched Raven and Kiva make themselves look like idiots because they defend your behavior every time someone says something. But I've never once seen you prove them right. No. You prove me right. Every single time. You're nothing but a spoiled jerk. You're not special because you can do magic or because you're half elf. You're just like us. You're a Squire. And if you don't want to suffer alone, you're going to learn to act like you want to fit in. Comprende?"

Crow sat stunned. He was unsure if he should respond. He looked around the table, Condor and Raven were also seated in silence. For a brief moment none of them moved. The tension could be cut with a metaphorical knife.

It was at that same moment, all of the Squire's phones, watches, and other technology began notifying them of the next test. The Squires were to be paired off for a competition which would see them travel to Mars in a standard Jump Pod. In order to pass, they simply needed to arrive. This did not seem too harrowing a task.

Crow was less than thrilled by the last sentence of the notification: "Your partner will be Penguin."

Crow excused himself. He quickly marched back to his room, plopped on to the bed and let his thoughts slowly collect. Had Crow been as terrible to Raven and Penguin as his brother to him? Why did Raven come to help him? Was he the same villain as his family?

"Numcustos Bestia!" He called out.

A door opened up in front of the bed. Numcustos walked into the room carrying an iced drink.

"How can I help ya Crow?"

"Am I a bad person?"

"You're literally seeking counsel from a Demidemon from Gehenna about whether or not you're a good person. Ask yourself is that something good people do?"

"No" Crow said dejectedly, "I don't think it is."

"Then you'd be wrong." Numcustos said.

"Everyday, you have an opportunity to decide who you are. Good isn't a permanent state of being. Good is a choice. You can be better. If you want. But

I don't care one way or the other. You're powerful and that's what is important to me." Numcustos said, "But I'm trying to become a powerful demon. You're trying to be a Crow."

Chapter 25

The message they received was a lie. Crow and Penguin were on a Jump Pod, a small metal spherical transport. Jump Pods were used mostly for terrestrial travel but they could handle short interplanetary trips such as the journey from Earth to Mars when properly fueled and maintained.

This Jump Pod was not properly fueled nor maintained. Instead, Crow and Penguin were floating in space. A hologram appeared in the ship. It was The Drakon King, he seemed to be sitting behind a table.

"By now you've seen that your fuel lines snapped about three quarters of the way to Mars. So, at the rate you're going it'll take a while to get there. I hope you brought plenty of supplies. I'm unsure if you knew this or not but it used to take years to get to Mars."

"We don't have days' worth of food, let alone years." Crow shouted angrily.

"It's a prerecorded message." Penguin said calmly.

"You have three choices. You can stay here until we send someone to get you." The Drakon King pulled a knife from somewhere out of frame and stabbed the table, "You can make your way to Mars."

Crow frowned. The second option was clearly the most difficult, but it was likely also the best way to pass.

"Or," The Drakon King said, "You can surrender knowing that you'll have failed the test for you and your partner. Whatever you choose, good luck."

The hologram of The Drakon King disappeared. Crow and Penguin sat in their chairs, stunned.

"We should obviously try to get to Mars."

"Obviously," Penguin argued, "we should stay here. The Jump Pod as it stands right now will not make it to Mars."

"But if we float along in space alone, we might be here for days, even years."

They argued to a stalemate, each person remaining technically correct but no closer to an actual solution. After a short while, the conversation turned to yelling and the yelling turned to silence. Crow was infuriated at the prospect of not getting his way. Before he could voice another idea, a hologram appeared where The Drakon King had been.

"Penguin, it's Raven. Hey Condor and I just got this crazy message from The Drakon King. Now we're..." Raven appeared on the monitor next to the Dwarven Mage. As tall as Raven looked by comparison, the Dwarf looked much more intimidating.

"Floating in space," Penguin interrupted, "we got it too."

"I figured as much. But I think we have a plan but we'll need Crow and Owl's help."

"Get Owl on the call then." Penguin said.

Owl appeared next to Raven and Condor. Beside her was a gigantic green humanoid with extended canine teeth and goat-like horns. By the scale of Orcs, this one was larger than Orc-Elf or an Orc-Man making him a classic Orc. Crow could only imagine the smell in Owl's Jump Pod.

"Someone please tell me how to fix these pods. I'm sharing with Ostrich. Not that there's anything wrong with Ostrich. We would never say anything bad about an Orc Berserker that can puncture a hole in the Jump Pod I'm in."

"I am stronger than the ship pod." Ostrich said in the background. "I am so strong, I can breathe in space."

"You are so strong." Owl said in a panicked, yet soothing tone.

"I have a plan," Condor spoke up. "First, Crow, can you summon A Black Rail?"

"I've never heard of it." Crow answered.

"It's a giant Creature in Dwarven Lore. Legend says that the Black Rail's took the place of trains to eat Dwarves that would use tunnels to escape their daily tasks."

"Numcustos Bestia!" Crow shouted, A door opened in the middle of the hologram and out stepped Numcustos. He instantly shielded his eyes from the light.

"What do you need boss?"

"Have you heard of a Black Rail?"

"Giant Worm Creature? Can disguise itself as a train? Can manipulate itself?"

"That's it!" Condor said excitedly.

"We don't have one." Numcustos said plainly. "Way too much up keep."

"I guess that'd be too convenient." Raven said.

"I have another idea." Condor said.

"What is it?" Everyone said in unison.

"We go through Crow's Gehenna Gate."

The dead silence of space was louder than the inside of the ship at the suggestion of going through a Gehenna Gate.

Chapter 26

During their first days at the academy, Squires were taught the basic principles of Magical Law. In addition to language, art, and arithmetic, the students on the Path of the Squire were all required to have an understanding of Magical Law beyond that of most adults. Raven, in his younger years had been no different.

The first law was that teleportation magic was illegal in every circumstance. This was because teleportation without a magical doorway required a living sacrifice. In the time before magical doors, Mages were known to carry rats and snakes as the necessary sacrifice. Towns on Earth with large Mage populations were littered with dead rats that were bred only to use as fuel for short distance teleportation. Disease ran rampant amongst humans. This became known as the Teleportation Illness, later known as the Bubonic Plague. The punishment for using Teleportation Magic was at minimum one Earth-year in prison. Teleportation Magic at a greater distance would require a larger sacrifice and therefore could also constitute a murder charge. Raven, as someone without magical abilities only learned this law for the sake of his Knighthood.

The second law was that no person was to use magic beyond their capability to handle. This law was created specifically to halt the creation of Noughts. Though uncommon on Earth, Noughts were the reason entire civilizations had been wiped from existence. Raven, had only ever seen one Nought, the Ice Nought that Crow had captured. By capturing the Nought alive, Crow had spared it the fate that most Knights awarded to Noughts, death.

The third law concerned Magical Realms. This was not truly a law so much as a warning. Not unlike placing a toaster oven in a bathtub. Yes, it was perfectly legal, though doing it almost always meant a painful death. No one should travel into a Magical Realm. Of course, there were hundreds of brave adventurers throughout history that had gone into Magical Realms and lived.

There were other laws but they were almost always derivatives of the first lesson Raven could remember. Though Condor's plan wasn't necessarily illegal, it was much more dangerous than anything anyone else would ever think of. The laws of magic were at their core, installed to ensure Mages wouldn't commit accidental suicide.

The Squires sat in a silence, the likes of which could only be achieved in the vacuum of space.

"You want to go through a Gehenna Gate?" Raven was the first to speak after what felt like an eternity.

"Yes" Condor answered plainly. "It's not as much of a suicide mission as you might think it is."

"So, it is a suicide mission," Penguin said. She was visibly frustrated.

On the front facing monitor, a Jump Pod was moving again. Seeing the Pod hurtling toward Mars filled Raven with a sense of dread. It suddenly hit him; the point of the test was never to make it to Mars. Instead, they were being tested on their ability to work together. A single out Jump Pod without fuel would never make it to Mars. The pairings in the pods were also almost all incompatible. Yet with all of that, the comms for the pods all functioned perfectly. They were supposed to help each other.

A second Jump Pod took off. It was moving through space as ungracefully as a Star Angel with a broken wing. Raven changed the view on the monitor.

"Okay guys, I don't mean to be pushy but other pods are moving." Condor said.

"We need to make a decision now. You must see what's happening. The test is either of our ability to survive with a team or work with a team to achieve our goal."

"Forget it, we're all going." Crow yelled into the comm before hanging up.

Doors opened in front of the Pods. Before Raven could process what was happening, the Pod was pulled into the door.

Everything felt uncomfortably warm and moist. Raven looked over at Condor. The blue Mage's crest under the Dwarf's eye was glowing. The hologram of Crow also had a glowing crest. Small spots under Penguin's hologram's left eye gave her the appearance of fluorescent freckles.

"Everyone." Crow's Hologram said, "Shut off your external monitors. Turn off any lights."

The order came too late. Pods seemed to disappear leaving Raven and Condor standing on what could only be described as a wasteland. The sky was as red as the cracked, dry, ground beneath them. The two Squires were between two cliff peaks that towered above them. Carved into the cliff walls were a series of tunes that were glowing blue not unlike the Mages' crest.

Suddenly a gigantic shadow cast itself over them. A large green reptile with dozens of eyes on its face and underbelly. Wrapped around the reptile's forelegs were red cloths that hung down over the cliff like flags. On the other cliff a similarly gigantic orange reptile with dozens of eyes began scaling down the wall. In front of them a third reptile, this one blue, was walking toward them.

Raven reached for his beam sword and to his dismay, it was not there. It was at that point he realized he was wearing his regular clothes, not his armor. Condor was wearing a typical Dwarven tunic and pants, outside his armor his long beard went down to his waist.

"You cannot use weapons here." The voice was unlike any Raven had heard before though it felt familiar. A door as large as a castle gate opened in front of them. Out stepped a gigantic biped that stood at least three stories tall. It had the legs of a goat, a burly torso clothed in a shirt and sport coat. Dangling from its neck was a bird cage, though Raven couldn't tell what was in the cage. Its head had an almost human quality to it though it had massive bull-like horns protruding from its head.

"I said no weapons." The giant said. All of Raven's weapons except his Anti-Magic imbued coins suddenly faded into nothing.

"Stand back" Raven shouted.

"I'm so scared." The giant said, feigning a shaking motion, "that was sarcasm. My morning constitution was bigger than you."

"Excuse me sir, what do you want?" Condor said.

"I like that one." The giant said, changing his gaze to Condor. "I'll eat you first"

"That's enough Numcustos." Crow shouted as he came into view from behind the giant. He was walking with the rest of their group, coming around the base of the cliff.

Raven's jaw dropped. He had seen the Demidemon dozens of times, it had never been a giant.

"Numcustos Bestia!"

The giant and the reptiles all stopped dead in their tracks. The giant turned its head a full one hundred and eighty degrees presumably to look at Crow.

"Crow. If I didn't absolutely need your magic when you die, I would leave you to your own devices." The giant said as its body contorted and shrank down to the size Raven was accustomed to.

"You would get bored and be back by tomorrow."

"Yeah, you're probably right." Numcustos said.

"How did you do that?" Raven asked.

"I'm a Demidemon. This realm is a magical fountain. I can do anything here."

"And what exactly is this realm?" Condor asked.

"It's Crow's Plane of Gehenna." The Demidemon said in an almost braggadocios tone, "It's where I go when I close a door. The real question I have is why are you all here?"

"We're traveling to Mars. Our ships died." Ostrich said. The Orc seemed to be the only one in their group unbothered by their circumstances.

"Really. I ask for an explanation and that's the best you've got." Numcustos said glaring at Ostrich, "You have been warned not to do this since you were five years old. But wait you're an Orc. You're a descendant of Gehenna. You should be fine. As long as you're a Mage."

"I am not a Mage."

"Well then you're going to die like everyone here but Crow." Numcustos said, "The Magic in this realm will over power you and you'll all turn into Beast Noughts. Then you'll be part of my zoo."

"Not the plan." Crow said.

"We need you to open a door to Mars." Raven said.

"There's a problem with your plan."

"That's it. Numcustos Bestia I've had enough." Penguin said. She marched in front of Numcustos, grabbed him by the collar and lifted him off the ground. "You're going to tell us how we're going to get to Mars."

"Whoa whoa. No need to threaten your favorite Demidemon." Numcustos said, "I can open the door. You're just going to fall fast and hard if you go

104

through it. The only door I have on Mars was in an a ship that didn't land."

"I'm not worried about that. I can use Enhancement Magic to shield us from damage." Owl said. Before she was even done talking, Raven could see her measuring everyone with her eyes. She wasn't exceptionally graceful with her spell casting, but she was quick. Before Raven knew what was happening, he felt his skin tighten. All of the Squires took a metallic quality to their skin and clothes."

"Open the door." Owl said, "We have three minutes."

Chapter 27

Crow was in a crater. Nothing hurt, though he was afraid to move. Magic was amazing. There was no way he would have survived the fall without it. He thought back to watching how fast Ostrich dropped from the sky. How Penguin said curses in the air that revealed the one thing she was afraid of, heights. Contrary to Penguin, Raven and Owl seemed to enjoy their free fall. The two laughed as they dropped from the sky. Crow couldn't help but think how much fun it would have been if they were in different circumstances.

Mars was a terraformed planet. At one point in human history, a trip to Mars was the experience of a lifetime. A few decades after being terraformed, it was discovered that Mages born on Mars almost exclusively had Earth, Water, or Animal magic. Soon after, Mars was the largest farm in the The Milky Way.

"Hey!" The voice came from a lime green skinned alien, "What have you done to my crops."

"We're Squires in the Knights of the Flock," Penguin said as she crawled out of the crater she left in the ground, "We apologize for the damage we've done to your crops"

"Wait did you say, Squires?" The Martian took his hat off and threw it in the air. His head had two sets of antennae on his head, for whatever reason, seeing a person with antennae made Crow think of Kiva.

"Yes." Penguin said.

"I'm rich!" The farmer shouted. "The king offered a reward for everyone that assists a Squire."

The farmer led the group to his truck and explained that all Squires were to be brought to the Capital Building. Conveniently it was only a five-hour drive from where they were. The farmer piled them into his truck. Ostrich was seated in front leaving Crow, Raven, Condor, Owl and Penguin all in the backseat or in the carriage of the truck. About two hours into the journey, Crow decided that this was the most uncomfortable thing he'd ever done.

An hour into the journey, Crow rotated to the carriage where several bumps in the road caused Raven to bounce on top of him.

"Alright," Crow shouted as he kicked Raven off of him, "I'm over this."

Crow waved his hand in a very specific pattern; a magical door opened beside the truck. A loud roar could be heard as the Gehenna Beast came bounding out beside the truck. The Gehenna Beast used two antennae to grab Crow and place him on its back. Similarly, Owl cast a spell that enhanced her speed to that of the truck and jumped out.

The remainder of the journey was much smoother on the back of the Gehenna Beast, though Crow's compatriots certainly seemed intimidated by the snarling cat monster.

After traveling through what felt like an endless field, the truck stopped in front of a one-story building in the center of a field of rice. Outside the building were two Knights of the Flock in full armor. The truck came to a stop, Crow returned the Gehenna Beast, and Owl disabled her spell.

"Well." The farmer said, "Here we are."

"I expected the capital to be more capital-y." Penguin said with a hint of disappointment in her voice.

"More land for farming I guess." Ostrich said, "An honorable way to use your land."

"I thought so too." The voice came from Hummingbird as she walked out of the building. Behind her was Blue Jay and Goose.

"Brother" Ostrich said to Goose.

"Brother," Goose replied, "You failed to distinguish yourself again. We're not reviewing you. You're taking the next phase of the test."

Ostrich looked down at his feet in a manner that was very much against every action Orcs were known to do in front of Elves and humans. Crow wondered if Goose and Ostrich were actually brothers or if it were an Orcish colloquialism.

"Actually," Hummingbird said, "they all distinguished themselves. Any pairing that elected to stay and be rescued failed. We purposefully placed you in pairs that we knew would lead to arguments."

"Passing isn't distinguishing." Goose said, "This round was stupid."

"It was not stupid." Blue Jay said, "None of these recruits are for The Party. But I might say that everyone here did something unexpected. They went through a magical dimension and came out rather unscathed."

"I want this one for The Charm." Hummingbird said while pointing toward Owl. "Her enhancement magic held up after a six mile fall."

"I want her." Goose said, "Imagine having my team be immune to damage."

"I thought you wanted Penguin." Hummingbird replied.

"I had the last Penguin. Of course I want this one. But I'm not sure."

The previous Penguin, Penguin and Puffin's grandfather was a renowned Knight of the Flock. He'd been on the Charm when it was The Wake under the previous Vulture. He'd elected to stay in the Flock to assist with Hummingbird's transition despite Hummingbird's obvious philosophical differences to the deceased Knight Commander. Every Squire learned about Penguin's exploits. He was the Knight that ended multiple civil wars on small planets without so much as the ability to magically light a flame.

"Well until you pick, everyone will move to the next round."

Chapter 28

Planet Mos, systems away from the Test of Might, a large man with sharp fangs, white hair that flowed between spikes running down his back and red eyes was working alone in a morgue. At his feet were the fresh corpses of the scientists that were assigned to work there. The man reached down and plucked the eyeballs from the nearest corpse and dropped it into a pouch that was tied to his belt.

"Silverback!" A voice rang in the man's head. "Begin the ritual."

"Begin the ritual." The man called Silverback said.

He opened every drawer until he found the bodies of three children. Silverback clumsily threw the children's corpses on the ground. He didn't need to be careful, this wasn't necromancy, an unaccounted bruise wouldn't cause them to become NRLs.

"Asleep the weak, awaken the beast." The voice in his head said.

Silverback leaned down to the three corpses and spoke the phrase "asleep the weak, awaken the beast." into each of their ears. He reached into his mouth and pulled out three fangs. He dropped a fang on each of the children.

"Are any of them Mages, Silverback?"

"Are any of them Mages, Silverback." Silverback repeated.

Silverback examined the three children. None of them had a Mage's Crest.

The children began convulsing. They screamed and cried as they came back to life. Their eyes opened as their hair began losing color until it was white. By the time the children started screaming, their mouths visibly fanged, their eyes were an unnatural shade of red. A red seal began forming around their left eyes. The seal developed incredibly quickly, these children were willing. It was perfect.

"We are all Beast Knights. We are all servants of The Chimera King." The voice in Silverback's head said.

"We are all Beast Knights. We are all servants of The Chimera King." Silverback and the children howled.

After a few hours of the children struggling to relearn how to walk, use their arms, stand, and most importantly, not wail, Silverback felt they were prepared to walk around the surrounding city.

So it came to pass, Silverback, a large human with long white hair and red eyes, walked around the city early in the morning followed by three children with white hair and red eyes dressed in the blood-soaked clothes that they died in.

"Do you have names?" The voice in Silverback's head said. As always Silverback repeated it out loud. This time the voice was only talking to him. This was how he preferred it.

"My." The tallest child spoke. "My. Name. Is. Lioness." Lioness was thin with wild hair that seemed to stick out in every direction. As she stood there, color began to return to her hair and skin which both had taken a grey-brown quality. Her eyes had a wild quality to them as if she was actively plotting against everyone. Surprisingly, she developed a second red seal under her right eye.

"My." The second child spoke. "My. Name. Is. Mink." Mink had long braided hair, not unlike Silverback. Her nails were long and colorful. She spoke in a hushed tone barely above a whisper.

"My name is Kuma." The third spoke as a voice in their heads. Kuma was a large child. Despite being shorter than

"Out. Loud."

"My." Kuma said, "My name is Kuma."

Rain fell on them shortly after the trek began causing the children to stop and stare into the sky unblinking. It was as if they had never seen rain before despite the fact that land masses on Planet Mos experienced rain eight days out of ten. Lightning flashed in the sky above them. The children scattered around the street.

Silverback groaned. One by one he lumbered toward the cowering children and grabbed them by the backs of their necks and began carrying them to their destination. He wished the voice in his head would tell them to calm down. Instead, Lioness bit him, Kuma howled loudly, and Mink said, "drop me."

Silverback persisted. After thirty minutes of walking, they found themselves queued in line for the days off-world shuttle. When they reached the front of the line, Silverback unceremoniously dropped Lioness and Kuma to the ground while Mink managed to climb onto his back where it remained. Silverback leaned forward so that the teller could see them all.

"I need passage to the Solar System in the Milky Way Galaxy." The voice in his head said.

"I." Silverback started. It was a complicated sentence; he needed a moment to formulate the it. He wasn't sure why names of locations always gave him such difficulty.

"We need passage to the Solar System in the Milky Way Galaxy." Mink said. Was she instructed to speak by the voice, or was she acting on her own?

"Sure thing sweetie." The window attendant said to Mink before turning back to Silverback, "passage cards."

Silverback stared at the man without saying a word.

The window attendant stared back for a second before repeating himself, saying, "Passage cards."

Silverback continued staring.

"Money." The attendant said.

Silverback reached into the pouch tied to his waist, pulled out some of the contents, and plopped four wet, green eyeballs on the man's desk.

"Stop right there," Lioness said, "If you start any alarms, Silverback here will personally pluck your eyeballs out, murder everyone on whatever ship he's intelligent enough to pilot and then crash it into our destination."

The attendant motioned but suddenly stopped.

He shoved four tickets over to Silverback.

"Your ship is about to depart."

The children immediately ran off toward the ship while Silverback stared back at the man, wishing to say "can I have my eyeballs back?" It wasn't his master's will for him to make such a request.

Regardless, he snatched the eyes back and took off after the children. Their next stop would be wherever their master sent them.

Chapter 29

Upon their return to Earth, Mirai demanded that Raven, Crow, Penguin, and Condor join her and Kiva for "an evening of games and questionable uses of magic." Owl had been invited too, but she had to decline as Hummingbird sent her immediately to her post on Venus. Condor also declined as he had to report back to the Dwarven Colony orbiting Saturn. More importantly, he needed to call his wife and son.

This left Raven, Penguin, Crow and Kiva to entertain the Regent. They were to play Cards Against Magic. The game was a trick deck. Each card had a question printed on it, failure to answer a question would result in an unknown magical effect. Raven and Penguin had played this game with Penguin's mother while they were in the Academy. As a result of refusing to answer a question, Raven had a neon pink sign above his head for a full day.

Mirai drew her first card, "If I had to guess who in the room was a mass murderer, who would it be?"

She paused and looked at the room.

"I pick…" Mirai said, "Me. I mean I am the one with the knowledge of the future. I know how everyone dies. I've seen you all dead, thousands of times."

Raven was not shocked by Mirai's answer. She was fascinated by death, perhaps because she had seen so much of it. Perhaps she harbored a fantasy of actually killing someone. Raven was slightly repulsed by the idea himself. Perhaps it was this reason why he preferred the sword to the gun. If he had to kill targets, he preferred it to be more personal than at a distance.

"My turn," Kiva said as she drew her card, "who do I find most attractive in the room?"

"Crow," everyone in the room said in unison with the exception of Kiva and Crow. It was at that moment that Raven learned Aesopians skin turned a teal blue when they blushed. Crow smirked.

"I have never said that." Kiva said, "I'm not answering."

The word "chicken," floated over Kiva's head in neon letters. She crossed her legs and sat, appearing to be embarrassed.

"My turn," Penguin said, "Would I rather eat dog food or dog meat?"

"Who wrote these things?" Raven asked.

"I don't know." Mirai said with a wide grin on her face, "but they are hilarious."

"I'd rather eat dog food."

"My turn." Crow said, "If I wasn't my current career what would I be?"

"Tough one," Mirai said, "I bet Crow would be a doctor?"

Raven reached forward and grabbed a chip from the bowl on the table. He knew the answer, it wasn't a doctor.

"I'm not answering."

A flash of purple light flashed and filled the room. Crow and Kiva immediately fell out of their chairs and to the floor. "What was that?"

"Oh man, I am so jealous of that card." Mirai said, "It causes you to switch bodies with the last person to fail to answer for six hours."

"Six hours." Crow and Kiva said in unison.

"Isn't it great." Mirai said.

Raven and Penguin couldn't hold in their laughter anymore. Crow stood up in Kiva's body.

"What's your problem Crow?" Raven said through laughter, "You finally can appreciate your own reflection."

"Shut up!" Kiva's mouth shouted. "Numcustos Bestia!"

Nothing happened.

"You won't be able to cast your spells like this. Imagine a child playing with an adult, you wouldn't want them having access to power they can't control."

"Fair enough." Crow's body said. The cross-legged pose that Kiva had assumed was so much more relaxed than Raven knew Crow was capable of. Meanwhile Crow in Kiva's body was extremely rigid and visibly uncomfortable.

"Okay, screw this." Crow said as he stood up in Kiva's body so quickly that the cards on the table were knocked to the floor.

"What is your problem?" Penguin yelled at Crow as he stood up.

"I woke up this morning with my body and now I don't have it. Now I have to use the bathroom and I have no idea how that works now."

"The same as anyone else." Kiva shouted back with Crow's mouth.

"Aesopians aren't that different from Earthlings," Mirai said between bursts of laughter.

"That's it! I have had enough of these games." Crow grabbed Kiva by the hand and pulled her with him as he stormed back toward his room, "You're not going to leave my sight for the next six hours."

Even though it was under Kiva's control, Crow smiling was a bit unsettling.

Once Crow and Kiva left the room, Mirai paused.

"Finally," Mirai sighed.

"Finally, what?" Raven asked.

"Those two are going to have a talk about three hours into their punishment." Mirai said with a devilish grin across her face, "in bed."

"Finally." Penguin echoed.

"Good for them," Raven said, "maybe Crow will relax a bit now."

"He doesn't." Mirai answered.

Chapter 30

It had been nearly three weeks and there still wasn't notice about what the next phase of the test would be. Crow would spend his days pacing back and forth trying to decipher what would be asked of him. Invariably, Kiva would make him sit down. He would sit for a few moments before getting back to pacing.

This was domestication. He wasn't upset at the latest development in his life, but it was strange. Crow had generally thought about himself. Yet here he was, doing things to make Kiva happy. It was all such a foreign concept.

Crow was in his thirtieth lap around his room when he received an email from The Drakon King himself: Squire Crow, please come to the courtyard at your earliest convenience. As you know, time is no issue for me.

He immediately stopped pacing and began moving toward the courtyard. The courtyard was a beautiful to people that enjoyed nature. Kiva and Crow spent nearly every afternoon since their adventures in each other's bodies. The grass was perfectly manicured. Each tree, every flower, and all of the shrubs were perfectly maintained as if frozen in time.

Crow did not enjoy nature.

The Drakon King was seated on the ground with his legs crossed. He was wearing a suit with a gold tie. Beside him was a novel with a bright red cover.

Crow immediately felt under dressed in his Jiu Jitsu Gi pants and t-shirt.

"Crow."

"Your highness."

The Drakon King smiled. "There really is no need to be so formal."

"So, what should I call you?"

"Honestly," The Drakon King said as he leaned backward, "I don't know. The ritual to become King erased my name from history. Just like nobody remembers what your name was before you were Crow."

"In fairness sir," Crow said, "I've been Crow about as long as I care to remember."

They shared a laugh. The Drakon King must have been aware of Crow's upbringing.

"So," The Drakon King asked, "you're wondering why I brought you here?"

He was.

"I just assumed it had something to do with the test and why we are awaiting orders."

"How perceptive." The Drakon King said. He lifted his hand off the ground, a flower sprung up where his had been resting.

"So, may I ask what is happening?"

"Mirai had a vision about the final section of the test. I'm running an experiment."

"You're seeing if you prolong the third section of the test past the planned start date, if it will still happen."

"Exactly." The Drakon King said, "You know, you could be an excellent Royal Guard one day."

"Thank you, sir." Crow said, unable to conceal his smile, "so what did Mirai see?"

The Drakon King frowned. "She saw an attempted Coup de tat. Sometimes it's successful, sometimes it isn't."

"So why don't you arrest the people that do it?"

"Because, it is a crime they haven't done yet. Do you know the implications of judging someone for a crime that hasn't happened yet. It's be catastrophic. Besides that, Mirai is the only living person with naturally occurring future sight. That's a lot of trust in her."

Crow frowned. As per usual, The Drakon King was right, they had no right to punish people for crimes "So how do you know it'll happen for sure?"

"One of our Knights was already attacked by one of theirs."

"Why are you telling me all this?" Crow asked.

"Because of everyone involved in the coup, you are conspicuous by your absence." The Drakon King said. "There is no future where you are involved. But you are visually conspicuous."

Crow's body language stiffened, "What's that mean?"

"I really can't tell you more because I don't know more."

Crow frowned. Conspicuous by his absence meant that whatever Mirai saw, Crow was now a suspect.

"Anyway," The Drakon King said, "You have a Gehenna Beast, would you like to see another magical creature?"

"What do you have in mind?" Crow said, trying to mask the concern on his face.

"I am in possession of a Thousand Year Dragon."

Crow stopped everything he was thinking about Mirai's vision. A Thousand Year Dragon was among the rarest of all the Magical Beasts. Simultaneously extinct and plentiful, they lived beyond the normal plane of time and space. For a mere man, elf or otherwise to possess one would require an astronomical amount of power.

"You're lying." Crow said without thinking whom he was speaking to.

"Goodness," The Drakon King said with a smile, "nobody has taken that tone with me since I was your age."

Crow shrunk back. He remembered his place and said, "I apologize your excellency."

"No need." The Drakon King said, "You should be able to say what's on your mind. Besides, if we're being honest, all the formality is exhausting."

"So where is it?"

"Here," The Drakon King stuck his hand out as a large, silvery-white egg materialized.

"Well, that can be any kind of egg." Crow said. While he didn't hatch many of his Beasts, he was familiar with hundreds of egg varieties.

"Look up." The Drakon King said while pointing up.

The sun was completely covered by what Crow at first assumed was cloud cover. Instead, it was an intimidation of silver dragons flying over the courtyard before disappearing completely almost as quickly as they appeared. Crow couldn't make out small details about them. Legends said that Thousand Years Dragons were beautiful and terrifying. But they were now all gone. All except for the egg in The Drakon King's hand.

"They're drawn to me." The Drakon King said, "They believe that I am one of them because I can use Time Magic and Space Magic as they can. The Thousand Years Dragons sometimes suddenly appear here, then leave."

"Why are you telling me this?" Crow asked.

"Because, it is rare that I encounter a half-elf like myself." The Drakon King said, "I really just wanted to make sure that you know, that I don't believe that you are capable of true evil."

With that, The Drakon King disappeared. As Crow started to walk away, he found a small sphere in his pocket. He now had a Dragon Egg in his possession. The Drakon King must have stopped time and placed it there.

"Numcustos Bestia!" Crow shouted out.

A door opened where The Drakon King had been previously standing. Numcustos swaggered out. His little three-piece suit was a light shade of blue instead of its normal pinstripe motif.

"Master of Beasts at your service."

"Are we equipped to hold a Dragon?" Crow asked.

"How large?" Numcustos asked, "How much roaming space does it need?

"I don't know?"

Numcustos frowned. "You know Crow. There is a lot of effort that goes into Dragons. If you're saying we're going Dragon hunting, then I'm going to say no. We are not equipped for a Dragon. Dragons are the original Mages; except they don't have inhibitions. We will die. Even if we managed to capture the Dragon, it'd be imprinted on its mother and the mother would come destroy us. In fact…"

"Numcustos!"

"Sorry for rambling. We aren't ready for a Dragon. Why are you wasting your time trying to capture a Dragon, you should be trying to capture a Leviathan."

"I am not saying we're hunting a Dragon." Crow said.

Numcustos's eyes widened. "What are you saying Crow?"

"I have a Dragon egg." Crow said with a satisfied grin.

"What kind of Dragon egg?" Numcustos tone quieted to a whisper.

"A Thousand Year Dragon." Crow said as he pulled the egg from his pocket to show Numcustos.

Numcustos snatched the egg.

118

Numcustos started grabbing at Crow's arms. "You have a Thousand Year Dragon."

"Is it legit?" Crow asked.

"Let me show you."

Numcustos opened a door to Crow's plane of Gehenna and began to walk through. Except for his arm which couldn't cross through. It was as if the egg was blocking his ability to enter.

"Why wouldn't the egg enter. Aren't you the master of beasts?"

"Yes and no. Most magical beasts, especially most dragons, originate from Gehenna. But some originate from Elysia. Some originate from other places."

"But you aren't technically entering Gehenna?" Crow asked confused.

"Close enough." Numcustos said as he tossed the egg back to Crow. Crow caught it and scowled at Numcustos. Numcustos shrugged and continued walking about the room as if he hadn't just casually tossed a fragile, priceless treasure.

"So, what am I supposed to do with this?"

"Your egg, your problem." Numcustos said, "Aren't you some sort of magical prodigy? Open a portal to a plane of Elysia."

"I don't think that I can do that." Crow said. He had never thought about opening a door to another plane. He tried. Nothing happened. It was as if there was nothing connected to where he wanted the door to.

"Well," Numcustos said, "did you do it?"

"No."

"Like I said," Numcostos said, "your egg, your problem. I can start grabbing creatures from other realms, but not Elysia. Demons can't go there."

"Our problem." Crow said, "Numcustos Bestia, I compel you to research how I can open a portal to Elysia."

Numcustos Bestia's eyes glowed red.

"Hey Crow." Numcustos said, "The King of Gehenna, Rex Diaboli, the Big Guy, just contacted me. I don't have to do any of your orders regarding Elysia."

"Interesting." Crow said.

"Yeah, I guess it is. For what it's worth, I want to see that Dragon when it hatches."

Numcustos Bestia walked into the door as Crow received a message.

"Your third and final portion of the Test of Might will be a simple game of strategy. Squires against Senior Knights."

Chapter 31

After years of simulations, Raven was finally able to stand in a field on Homeworld, in the sun and relax. This had become an almost daily ritual for hours a day. He still trained and studied, but he made sure to take advantage of the opportunity to relax as often as time permitted.

Birds flew overhead. Crickets chirped. Insects flew around him. Raven stared up at the sky, hoping to see an actual raven fly across the sky. It hadn't yet happened, so he resolved himself to seek out his namesake once he finished the Test of Might as a reward for his efforts.

It was at this moment of tranquility that Raven was notified that the next section would be "a game of strategy" against his superiors.

Then the explosion happened.

A tower of the King's castle fell.

"Raven." His phone screamed at him. The voice was Penguin.

"What just happened."

"You need to get back to the castle it's…." The phone cut out.

"Penguin!" Raven shouted. "Penguin!"

"What's wrong Squire" A voice behind him said. Raven turned around to see Swan walking from a magical door.

"Swan." Raven said, "Thank goodness."

"There, there, it'll all be alright." Swan said, "Report."

"We're under attack."

"Have you seen the enemy?"

"Actually, I believe I have." Raven said as he reached across his belt and drew his beam sword.

Swan laughed out loud. She brushed her blonde bangs away from her eyes as a book floated from her bag.

"This is the test, isn't it?"

"So, you aren't the idiot that everyone thought you were."

Raven lunged in for a slash at Swan but was immediately bounced back as if he ran into a rubber wall.

"Well, you have no reservations."

Raven wasn't surprised his quick attack hadn't worked. Swan was the deadliest warrior in The Gaggle, the death squad. Though, when pictures from missions came back, Swan almost never had so much as a hair out of place.

"I don't need reservations."

"Raven." The phone shouted, this time it was Condor's voice, "wherever you're at get to…"

"Silence.

The great equalizer.

The strongest and the weakest,

all eventually fall to silence."

Swan recited the poem. Her book glowed neon green before Raven's phone went silent."

Raven held his hands out and tried to focus his energy into an Anti-Magic pulse. He briefly felt his hand go numb and the air around him begin to warm. Just as quickly as it started, it stopped.

"Did you just try Anti-magic on me?"

Raven didn't answer.

"You totally did." Swan said in a somewhat surprised sounding tone.

Raven turned for a retreat to the castle. This was the first time he regretted wearing the heavy armor.

Swan read from her book again as it began to glow.

"The leg of my enemy tried to run.

Each step driving him further into the ground.

Trapping him.

Swallowing him.

Soon he was hopeless."

Raven fell to the ground. He quickly picked himself up and tried another charge. This time he changed his footing so that when he was rebounded backward, he rolled instead of landing flat on the ground.

Swan's book glowed again. Raven couldn't hear what she said though as a magical door opened underneath him.

Chapter 32

Crow opened as many doors as he could. Squires against members of The Gaggle in a free for all was not the game of strategy that he'd pictured. Goose had already gotten a dozen or so Squires to surrender. Swan had restrained nearly double that number. The test had only been going for a few short minutes.

They were in a pocket dimension that Crow had intended to turn into a workshop. Raven fell to the floor.

"Where am I?"

"In my room."

"How long can we stay hidden?"

"Not long." Crow responded, "I'm sure Swan has a way of entering pocket dimensions."

Crow looked around at the twenty-seven people he had managed to transport. As it stood, this was about the maximum that he would be able to transport. Opening that many doors was something he hadn't done before. He reached his hand in his pocket and felt the egg; it was warm but unmoving.

"How many senior knights are there?"

"As far as we know, just two. Swan and Goose."

"That's all they need." Cassowary, an Orcman Squire said over everyone else.

The Squires erupted into chatter.

"Everybody shut up." Penguin yelled. "I have a plan."

The Squires silenced.

"Good." Penguin said as she walked around the room, "They aren't working together. They're just sowing chaos. Every test so far has really been about our ability to adapt to situations. This time the situation is an unwinnable conflict."

"So, what's your plan?" Another Squire shouted.

"We're going to get them to attack each other." Ostrich bellowed.

"No." Penguin said. She was visibly annoyed.

"We're going to face them in a rousing battle of strength against strength." Ostrich yelled while waving his fist.

"No." Penguin repeated. A vein was visible on her forehead.

"We need to solve the conflict," Crow said, "That doesn't mean we need to beat Goose or Swan in active combat."

"Exactly." Penguin said.

"So, what do we know about Goose and Swan?" Crow asked.

"Swan is arguably the strongest mage in all of the Knights of the Flock. Her magic is really an unknown since most people can only use one or two types of magic but she can use seemingly everything but time magic." Raven said. For once, Crow appreciated Raven's trivial knowledge of the Knight Commanders.

"Great." Penguin said, "What do we know about Goose?"

The entire dimension shook. Crow felt a sharp pain as if his teeth were being ripped out of his skull. Suddenly the room filled with light from the outside world.

"What do you want to know about Goose?" A deep voice said from the light, "I'm here."

Ostrich charged at Goose and actually knocked him down. Cassowary, Emu, and two other Orc Clansmen piled on top of the Knight Commander.

"Run." Ostritch yelled out, "We won't be able to hold him."

"All remaining Orc Clan pass."

The Orc Clan all disappeared into thin air. There was no flash of light. They didn't fade away. There was no sign of magic use. The Orc Clansmen just disappeared, clearly pulled into a parallel dimension.

Crow was faced with an immediate decision. He could collapse the pocket dimension completely and risk a battle with both Goose and Swan or a closed quarters battle with an Orc named "The Weapon of Mass Destruction" by the other squads.

"Collapse the dimension." Penguin shouted.

"But what if…"

"There is no time for butts." Penguin shouted, "Do it now"

Crow collapsed the dimension. In the time it took for him to blink, the Squires and Goose were in the courtyard surrounded by the burning castle. Crow was sweating before he realized the structure around him was burning. Under normal circumstances, he would question whether or not a mistake was made. Goose lunging for him only to be stopped by a split-second casting of 1000 Hands of the Needy, was not a normal circumstance.

Crow silently commanded the hands to constrict the herculean Orc. They anchored themselves to the ground, then to each other then gripped around his wrists and ankles. Against a normal man, it would have been enough to completely immobilize them. The hands were each empowered by the souls of their former lives as soldiers, murderers, assassins, and others that begged not to move on. Supposedly, they were only as strong or weak as their summoner required. Even still, Crow could feel a pressure emanating from Goose. Goose was radiating strength.

Crow's gaze met with the black, soulless eyes of the Orc Berserker. Crow felt as if all the hope was seeping from his body. He felt the need to beg for his life. It became an uncontrollable urge. Crow opened his mouth but was immediately interrupted.

"Crow it's a spell!" Condor shouted as he fired some sort of shoulder mounted cannon at Goose from behind.

Goose grimaced but didn't seem to be distracted from trying to free himself from the hands. With a mighty heave he was able to free his right arm. Crow started planning his next move.

"Good deduction, Condor." Goose said as he pulled himself free from the hands completely. The Orc leapt across the courtyard to Condor and punched the Dwarf in the chest.

Condor went flying through the air as if he had been hit point blank by a ballistic missile.

"You pass." Goose said. Condor disappeared as the Orcs did before him.

"Numcustos Bestia!" Crow shouted.

A door opened in front of Crow but before Numcustos could walk through it, a white light shone down on it.

"I can't come out." Numcustos said.

"What's happening?" Crow shouted.

An arrow went whizzing past his face as Penguin fired at a target on Crow's left. Swan was now on the battlefield.

"I don't know." Numcustos Bestia said as the arrow dropped out of the sky.

Chapter 33

Raven did not realize he had sent out an Anti-Magic pulse. He wasn't quite sure that he did it. Suddenly Goose dropped unconscious while Crow's 1000 Hands of the Needy disappeared. The flames on the castle dissipated. A Mage Squire that was flying above them plummeted to the ground. Luckily their armor would save them from physical harm.

Penguin launched herself past Raven and kicked Swan in the face. Swan grasped at her nose before the magic of the armor she was wearing healed her.

"Was that Anti-Magic?" Penguin yelled.

"I think so." Raven yelled back.

"Great job." Penguin yelled.

"I have no idea how I did that."

"Quick." Penguin shouted, "tie them down."

"You pass." Swan said with a teasing smile.

Penguin disappeared.

Goose stood up as if he were unbothered by everything.

"You two, Crow and Raven." Goose said.

"Its obvious that you're going to pass." Goose said before a wide grin spread across his face. It was terrifying, "I will pass you automatically right this second, if you turn on the rest of the Squires and join us."

Raven stopped. He didn't answer. He didn't know how to.

He wondered if this was a trick.

If it was a trick then Raven would surely have failed. If it wasn't though, years of training would be validated. He could have everything he ever wanted.

He had already disabled the magic of the mages and the other Squires were too injured or fatigued to raise a major concern, especially if Raven and Crow worked together.

He pondered, was this the opportunity that he deserved.

The thought that he could turn on his fellow Squires scared Raven.

"No." Crow said, "It isn't worth breaking the trust of my future squad mates."

"Good choice." Goose said, "You pass."

Crow disappeared. The rest of the Squires disappeared. Goose disappeared. Swan disappeared.

Raven stood in place, surrounded by the cold dead remains of the ruined castle. A Magical Door opened in front of him. From behind it, Tempest walked out. The tall slender elf clapped his hands.

"You passed Raven." Tempest said in his usual flat tone.

Raven breathed a sigh of relief.

"You didn't know if you were going to turn on your team did you?"

"I never was going to turn on them."

"But you considered it," Tempest said, "I can tell."

"I won't lie, Sir." Raven said.

"As you shouldn't." Tempest said, "Sometimes as a Knight, you will have to make a decision that is best for mankind. I would be disappointed if you didn't at least think about it. But do me a favor, the next time your future is on the line, do the option that gets you out of the situation safe. Too many young men die trying to be heroes."

"Yes sir." Raven replied.

"One day when you have to make a decision for the betterment of mankind, I hope you will make the better decision." With that, Tempest disappeared. The test of might concluded.

Chapter 34

Silverback was being patient with Lioness. She was better at communicating than the large Beast Knight. Anytime the group needed anything in their travels, Lioness did the talking. Any time they needed to communicate with their master, The Chimera King, Lioness took the most time. She always asked questions. Soon Mink and Kuma asked questions too. The Chimera King never seemed frustrated with the three new recruits. Instead, he always thanked them for the questions.

Silverback found himself fantasizing about collecting the children's eyeballs. He never threatened them, not that he knew how to verbalize a threat.

They were in a leaky shack on some planet that had rain seemingly every day. Originally, they had been ordered to Earth but when they arrived, The Chimera King personally met them and ordered them to another star system.

Silverback did not care where they went. It was the will of The Chimera King.

"Are we zombies?" Lioness asked Silverback.

Water dripped into a bucket Silverback set up next to him from the ceiling. He grabbed the bucket and drank it to stop overflow before it started.

"No." Silverback mustered the strength to say.

"Are we NRLs?" Lioness asked.

"No." Silverback repeated. "Same. Thing."

"What are we?" Lioness asked. Her eyes seemed to bulge when asking questions.

"Beast Knights."

"What. Are. Beast Knights?" Mink asked.

"Us." Silverback said. He reached into his bag of eyeballs to play with them. A few were drying out. He dunked the entire bag into the water bucket. Another hole in the ceiling must have formed because Kuma howled out loud as he was soaked.

"Why don't we use the money from Master to rent a nicer place instead of a shack?"

"Can't. Count." Silverback replied. "Can't. Talk."

"I can talk." Lioness said. "I can learn to count."

"You're. Not. Adult." Silverback replied.

"This shack is in a dangerous area."

"No. Isn't." Silverback argued.

Suddenly there was a rapping at their door. The children did as they were trained. They turned off any lights and hid in the shadows. Silverback stood up, bumping his head on the ceiling the process, and walked to the door.

"Told you." Lioness said.

What greeted him was a small blue skinned humanoid. A boy, he thought. Though identifying genders was not important to him. Lioness was very insistent that she and Mink be referred to as females.

"Help!" The boy screamed.

"No." Silverback said.

"You've got to help me."

"No."

Lioness emerged from the shadows and pushed Silverback out of the way. "What's wrong?"

"I'm being chased."

"Why?" Lioness asked.

"He stole my drug money" A larger blue skinned humanoid brandishing a jagged blade screamed at the group as he charged toward the boy. The boy immediately hid behind Silverback.

"What is drug money?" Lioness asked.

Silverback did not know the answer. He changed his gaze to the man in front of him.

"I'll tell you later, help me." The boy said.

"No." Silverback said.

"Good on you, big guy. Give me the boy." The man said.

"No." Silverback said.

A crowd of tougher looking blue skinned humanoids began forming around the doorway to the shack.

"Give me the boy and nobody gets hurt." The humanoid.

"No." Silverback said. He wasn't defending the boy. The humanoid with the blade seemed to be threatening and as a Beast Knight, Silverback was forbidden from responding to threats or orders from anyone other than The Chimera King or a superior Beast Knight.

Lightning cracked across the sky.

"Big mistake." The blue man said, "if you don't give him over right now, I'll just take him and then go in your shack and leave no survivors"

"No."

"Wrong choice," The man said as he lunged forward with the blade and plunged it into Silverback's stomach. Silverback twitched. This was supposed to hurt. It may have hurt him if he weren't a Beast Knight. Before the man could react to his own failure, Silverback grabbed him by the throat, lifted him up a full arm's length, and slammed him down onto the wet ground.

Silverback kept his gigantic hand around the man's throat. He kept gaze with the man as the blue of his skin turned into a deep purple before the man stopped twitching. He then reached for the blade in his stomach and used it to cut the throat of the nearest threat.

"No survivors" Silverback said. Lioness nodded in response. The children went flying forward out of the shack to the apparent horror of the blue skinned boy. They proceeded to all of drug dealers. All attempts to fight back or escape were utterly futile.

Mink struck first. She climbed up a man's back and bit his corroded artery. Blood sprayed on the ground. Her next victim was a woman whom tried to fire a weapon at the smallest Beast Knight. Again, the weapon failed. Mink pulled the bullet out of her shoulder, put it in her mouth and spat it back at the woman nearly as fast as it had been initially fired. When she missed the shot, her fingernails elongated like claws, and she stabbed the woman in the throat.

Kuma's first victim was smaller man whom he tackled to the ground and choked to death using the victim's own jacket collar. This was his strategy for his next several people.

Lioness did not kill as much as the other two. The victims she did kill were perhaps the most impressive. Somehow, she had managed to awaken some sort of magical potential. She grew long white claws and slashed at a few of the victims that attempted fleeing.

When they returned soaked in blood, rain, and tears, the children stared at the blue skinned boy whom was paralyzed with fear. Lioness reached into the bag on Silverback's waist and dropped several fresh eyeballs. Silverback did not care that they were from Lioness, they were new toys.

The boy fell to his knees and begged for his life unintelligibly. His face soaked from rain, tears, and splashed blood.

Silverback halted the attack, "Can you count?" He asked the boy.

Chapter 35

Puffin was proud that his first day out of medical attention was the graduation ceremony for the Squires. He donned his armor and cape. It was bittersweet because he was not allowed to be a part of the Test of Might.

The ceremony was held in the theatre in the Flock Ship Hercules. Hercules was the biggest ship in the entire fleet. The theatre was designed for any type of live performance. The stage was large enough for three full orchestras with screens above it that showed what was happening on stage. Above them, behind them, and on the floor were hundreds of thousands of individual LEDs and three-dimensional projectors that allowed the set to be anything for any performances. The stage was going to be ornate with the seals of The Drakon King and the Knights of the Flock floating around the Squires. When the Squire's name was read, their new Squad's seal would float alongside the other seals.

Additionally, The Drakon King had personally ordered a gift for each Squire. A lot of the time, these gifts were upgraded versions of the Squire's favorite gear. At Puffin's own graduation, he received a book of protection charms. The book added new pages as Puffin became more proficient in drawing runes. Even now, years later, he was still finding new pages added to the book.

Puffin was backstage waiting on his entrance queue. He was a surprise for the Squires whom had only been informed that he was injured in an attack prior to their test. He had not seen them since.

"I have some unfortunate news for you dear Squires." Hummingbird said, "The Drakon King is dealing with some business in another Star System and as much as he would like to be here, he had to send a replacement."

Puffin walked on to the stage to a roaring applause. He felt himself crying tears of joy before he could even reach the microphone.

"It's going to take more than a sneak attack to kill me." Puffin said. The Squires cheered again. A few months ago, most of them would knowingly skip his mission briefs, now he was receiving a hero's welcome, the likes of which he had not received since he was active in the field.

He began reading the names. Each name received a roaring applause from the Squires and the audience members.

Some of the Squires took their chance to gain extra attention while walking across the stage. The Orcs, Orcmen, and Orcelves all roared upon hearing their name called. All of them were called to the Gaggle. Each of them received heavy blunt weapons from The Drakon King. Puffin was not surprised by this. Most of them were Low Tier Knights, First Class.

Loon was also called to the Gaggle under Goose as a Low Tier Knight, Third Class. He laughed all the way across the stage. Puffin breathed a sigh of relief that he would never have to order Loon again. Loon's gift from The Drakon King was a gigantic scythe, the blade was made of yellow plasma.

Condor was assigned to The Party as a Mid-Tier Knight, First Class under Blue Jay. He received a fully stocked pocket dimension complete with a junkyard of old machines. Condor walked across the stage with his wife and two sons to great applause. His oldest son had a blue Mage crest on his eye that seemed to be flickering as if it could disappear at any moment. Puffin felt jealous of the boy's freedom to be whatever he wanted.

Owl was called to the Charm. She received a skin suit that would boost her own enhancement magic capabilities. She was now a Mid-Tier Knight, Second Class.

Penguin received a great applause when she was called. When she got across the stage, she shared a rare hug with her cousin, Puffin. They would be working together on The Charm. Penguin was noted to be starting on the Leadership Track. Immediately, she was promoted to Mid-Tier Knight, First Class. The same rank as Puffin. Her gift was a book of offensive charms.

Crow was accompanied across the stage by Numcustos Bestia. To the surprise of nobody, he was made a Mid-Tier Knight, First Class and assigned to Earth to be a Royal Guard. His gift was some sort of magical artifact, a tablet with some kind of strange writing. It made no sense to anybody but the

Demidemon that was riding on Crow's shoulder.

After a couple dozen names, the Squire that Puffin least expected to be there walked across the stage. Raven was also assigned to the Royal Guard, though he was only made a Mid-Tier Knight, Third Class, the bare minimum to be a Royal Guard.

"You actually get two gifts." Puffin said to Raven.

"I do." Raven said quizzically.

"Yes." Puffin answered before pulling out a custom Darkstar blade. This Darkstar blade was magically imbued so that it could change length and shape per the user's necessity. Puffin demonstrated by making it appear to be a katana.

The second gift came with a note from The Drakon King that read, "do not wear this on missions." Raven opened the box to find a black hat that looked exactly like the one he lost on Aesop. The crowd laughed and cheered as Raven put it on and did a quick dance before shuffling off to his seat.

For the Squires and for Puffin himself, this felt like a rare moment of happiness. There was no conflict. There was no stress. Even when Puffin felt a tug in the back of his mind to answer a voice that he had been ignoring in his head for months.

Act 3: The Second King

Chapter 36

One Earth standard year passed from the day that they graduated from Squireship.

Being a Royal Guard meant much less free time than being a Squire had ever afforded Crow. Often times as a Squire he had weeks or even months between missions, now he was going off every day. It got to the point where Crow began studying how to get his puppets to do easier missions in his spare time. Thus far they were moderately successful, though their reports lacked overall detail.

As a Mid-Tier Knight on a normal unit, he would have been a superior officer to most of the new Knights. Here, he was the second lowest ranking member. Tempest, his father, was the highest ranked as an Elite Knight First Class. Easter and Tornado were Elite Knight, Second and Third class respectively.

"Crow." A woman's voice shouted over the intercom in his quarters. It was Easter, the second highest ranked Knight in the Flock. Crow had only just laid down after a mission saw him travel with the Regent of Mars to a farming convention.

"Yes Lady Easter." Crow responded trying to mask the exhaustion in his voice.

"Come to the training area. You have some work to do."

Crow rolled off of his bed and dressed himself in black pants and a black shirt. He then pulled his braids into a bun and placed the Thousand Year's Dragon egg on his dresser before walking through the King's Castle. Eventually he made it to the training room, which was a large, empty, padded room.

Easter was in a way; the best mentor Crow could ever have had. She was half human-half elf. She was also regarded as a genius of Creation Magic. Not an exact translation to Crow's own Beast and Golem Magics, but it was close enough. Kiva, a user of Creation Magic herself was often verbally jealous of Crow's mentorship under Easter.

She was a tall woman with brown skin and long gray hair. Easter never removed her heavy armor or cape in public, so Crow had no idea what she looked like below her neckline. To display her magic, she was constantly orbited by glowing stones which she could manipulate into anything she chose, including magical doors. Everything Crow had ever read about Easter was that she had immeasurable power.

"Crow." Easter said. "Summon a Golem."

"Numcustos Bestia."

A magical door opened in between the two Royal Guards. Before Numcustos could emerge, the door slammed shut.

"I said you summon the Golem."

Crow frowned. This was an immediately exploitable weakness that Easter had honed in on their first meeting, he was too dependent on Numcustos Bestia for larger spells.

"Don't frown." Easter admonished him. "Summon a Golem."

Crow concentrated on opening a door large enough for a Golem to walk through. Nothing appeared.

"What will you do when you can't summon Numcustos to do your bidding."

"That's not something that could happen." Crow tried to explain, "We signed a contract. He has to come to my bidding, I have to help him become a full demon."

"He's a Demidemon. Every time you summon him, it costs you a bit of your life force. Even as an elf, you do have a finite life force. Elves die all the time."

"It's not that simple." Crow said.

"Why not?"

"Our magic is tied together."

"Then you need to stop using him as a familiar. It's not beneficial to you at all."

142

"What do you suggest?"

"Enthralling your familiar."

"Couldn't that kill me?"

"I honestly doubt it." Easter explained, "when they teach you magical laws it's because they are built around the average magic practitioner. You're not average.Just think about it."

Crow bowed and exited the room. He considered his circumstances with Numcustos Bestia. Enthralling Numcustos would permanently bind the Demidemon to the mortal plane and take away all of Numcustos's free will, he'd be more of a weapon than a living thing. Crow would no longer need to summon his familiar as a tether for other larger summoned creatures. In exchange, he would give Numcustos a small portion of his total life force. Hundreds of Mages had enthralled familiars, only to die shortly after. Ultimately, Crow decided it would not be worth it. Crow valued Numcustos as much more than a familiar, he was a friend.

When Crow returned to his room, he noticed the egg stir slightly.

Chapter 37

The Knights of the Flock generally employed three different kinds of ships though there were hundreds of variations of each. All ships were powered by a magical engine. The engines themselves were self-sustaining and self-cleaning.

The first were Residential Units, these were large ships that floated around space. Occasionally they were used for exploration but for the most part they moved in set patterns across galaxies. They were mostly designed for comfort and Knight Training. The Resolution, the ship that Raven and Crow were trained on, was one such ship.

The second were Transport Units. These were vessels designed to go from planet to planet. Journeys in these kinds of cases were designed to travel for short time periods of no more than seven weeks. A lot of these ships had weapons systems and even warp drives. Speeders and Jump Pods were technically Transport Units, though there was an argument for classing both kinds of smaller ships separately.

The third ship type were Destroyers. These were smaller than Residential Units but armed to fullest extent possible. One ship was enough to conquer an entire planet before deploying any soldiers. The Destroyer earned its name for being The Drakon King's chosen weapon against the Ganymeade Rebellion.

Raven was one of five thousand soldiers on Flock Destroyer X-3849, "The Mona Lisa." It was a routine joint exercise between members of The Gaggle, The Party, and The Royal Guards. In the event of some sort of conflict, it was best to patrol areas where conflict had risen before. Though the last time a conflict had actually occurred had been decades prior, Raven took this no less serious than if they were expecting a conflict that day. He leaned back in his chair on the Bridge in his newly customized black armor.

Chickadee, a human Squire that was known to be "too nice for this line of work." came up to Raven and asked, "Sir Raven, we have communication from Lord Tempest."

"Patch him through." Raven commanded.

"Raven my boy," Tempest began, "I want you to direct your ship at a 38-degree angle and travel 40,000 kilometers."

"What am I looking for?"

"An unregistered ship." Tempest said as he looked into the camera, "Actually several."

"Several unregistered ships. How many are we talking?"

"One Destroyer and four hundred Transport Units equipped for battle."

"That is not several, that is an army."

"They're heading toward Earth. Stop them."

A year ago, when he had first been promoted from Squire to Mid-Tier Knight, Raven would have rushed his ship into battle. Hundreds of hours of punishment at the hands of Tempest had taught him to be patient and attempt diplomacy.

Raven had the communication specialist sync signals up with the foreign fleet. A bead of sweat rolled over his brow.

"Attention unregistered ship fleet," Raven said, he stared into the monitor hoping for a response.

A dark grey face with ruby-red eyes appeared on the screen. The face had a red magical seal under its eye indicating it was likely a Mage or otherwise some sort of magically empowered. Raven wondered about what would make a magical seal turn red.

"We do not need to answer to you or your role."

"Yes, yes you do." Raven said, "identify yourselves or face imminent and irreparable consequences."

"Heretic, we follow only the laws put forth by the one true king, The Chimera King."

"And what does this Chimera King want?"

"The Chimera King only wants for everyone to follow him and unlock their potential."

"Send A-Squad to their location, light them up." Raven ordered.

A 12-ship group of transport vessels equipped for battle silently sped past the Mona Lisa. The monitor switched to a split screen between the The Chimera King's emissary and the leader of the A-Squad's ship.

A bolt of light fired through one of the A-Squad ships. The ship remained intact but it was floating aimlessly in space. Raven ordered a ship from B-Squad to go assist the pilot. The ship was stopped in the same method. A-Squad fired about 100 laser shots at the enemy. Thirty of their ships exploded.

"Emissary..."

"Bonobo"

"Emissary Bonobo, the last thing we want is for our destroyers to open fire. No one would survive."

"That is where you are wrong heretic, I am under orders to destroy everything en route to the Solar System."

Raven muted the monitors. A Squad wiped out one of their squadrons. Raven's mind immediately went to a simple fact, a battle featuring two destroyers always ended when a destroyer fired their nuclear fission cannon. Raven switched his strategy to preserving the most people rather than just stopping The Chimera King's army.

"Have all Mages open Magic Doors inside our ships that are still out there. We're going to fire the NFC."

"Sir, do you think that's necessary?"

"Yes." Raven replied, "they outnumber us twelve to one."

"Sir, look!"

"The defeated A-Squad ships had somehow restarted. Raven opened a third window on the monitor to speak to one of the defeated pilots, Goshawk. Goshawk, an elf with peach colored skin and shimmering blue eyes, was now a slate grey with red eyes.

"Goshawk," Raven said, "what's your status?"

Goshawk and Bonobo answered simultaneously, "You deserve no answer heretic."

"It appears to be some sort of spell." Chickadee said, "Sir the Mages are in place."

"Bring all our pilots in. Put any whose vessel was defeated in the air lock."

The door opened behind Goshawk on screen and sucked him in. Raven smiled, his friends' strategy from the Test of Might was now a widely accepted military tactic, though it was banned for civilians.

"Now fire!" Raven ordered.

In the vacuum of space there was no sound, on any planet, the sound was loud enough to be heard for miles in any direction. Even inside the Mona Lisa, it sounded like a screeching falcon as all the energy fired in one direction for 6 seconds. The cameras Raven had been viewing disappeared to static.

"Sir a report from the Airlock." One of the low tier knights said.

"Proceed" Raven replied.

"They're all grey now with that red seal."

"Are they NRL's"

"No." The Knight said, "there are no traces of Necromantic magic."

"Bind them. Then bring them back to Earth."

A year of training to remain calm couldn't hide Raven's frown. This was not the first experience the Knights of the Flock had with the Beast Knights but it was the most destructive with a cost of hundreds of ships. Looking at a monitor that was just a few minutes before, alive with lights and ships whizzing past the camera. Instead, he was now staring at endless darkness. The odd ship part would float by. But all it did was highlight that Raven had just ended thousands of lives in order to protect his Kingdom. He wanted to vomit. He wanted to send letters to the families of each of the deceased. But most importantly, he wanted to never make that kind of decision again.

Chapter 38

Puffin woke up, put his contacts in and his make up on. He stared into the mirror and frowned. He stared at himself in the mirror and longed for his old appearance, back when he was a rising star. Now he was tired.

"You know," the voice in his head said to him, "if you give in. I can make you look the way you used to."

"Tempting but still no."

His makeup smeared again.

"Eventually, you'll have to give in. You're becoming more and more like us every day."

"And that's why today we're going to exercise you."

Puffin pulled a marker from his desk drawer and placed it in his pocket. Then he pulled his rug up, revealing dozens of magical and alchemical symbols. It had been months to no avail. He drew a new symbol on the floor, then bit his thumb and used blood to activate the seal on the floor. The seal gave off a white light. Puffin passed out momentarily and woke up unchanged.

The voice in his head laughed menacingly. "That tickled."

"I hope you're having fun, spirit."

"I'll give you a hint. Your body is rejecting this because you've gone through a similar process. But you're going to be mine."

Puffin punched the floor; he couldn't figure it out.

There was a knock at the door.

Puffin scrambled to put the rug back and calm down enough to answer the door.

"Who is it?"

"It's me." The voice was Penguin.

"Oh, it's you." Puffin opened the door.

"So, what are you doing today?"

"Literally the same thing that I do every day, I'm trying to solve this affliction. The spirit that's haunting me gave me a hint today; I've been through this before."

"It couldn't be a Knight ritual, could it?"

The ritual to become a Knight of the Flock was the most expansive magical ritual that was performed on a regular basis. Children were led to an auditorium where they drank a tonic while a group of Mages cast a spell on them to enhance their strength, stamina, and magical capabilities. In exchange, the Knight's true identity was completely erased to everyone except blood relatives, even then, their names were lost forever anywhere it was written was replaced. Oftentimes, the new Squires would reject their families after the ceremony. The only way to break the ritual was for a knight to die.

"That's impossible."

"Hear me out," Puffin said, "What if I died."

"You did die." The spirit said, "clever for a human."

Puffin used his sleeve to wipe his makeup away. The red seal under his eye was fully exposed. He braced himself for Penguin's reaction. The Knights of the Flock had decided that corpses with the red seal were to be cremated immediately as it was apparently a form of necromancy; this was despite the fact that they didn't give off any necromantic energy.

Penguin took a step back and armed her wrist launched cross bow. "You're not going to eat me, are you?"

"I could make you eat her if you want." The voice in his head said.

"No." Puffin stammered, "I'm not going to eat you."

"Then I'm going to help." Penguin said.

Puffin's jaw dropped. He was positive that Penguin wouldn't accept him.

"You need to do your makeup better. You shouldn't be able to rub it off that easily. You're getting away purely because nobody wants you on field missions these days. I mean it makes way more sense, if you're a zombie, there's no way exorcism talismans and circles would work. My next thing would have been to call a Mage but you definitely can't do that."

Puffin was relieved. The two spent another couple hour trying to exercise

149

the spirit to no avail. Puffin wasn't as dejected as usual, telling Penguin made him feel better. It was as if a long-held weight was finally lifted from his shoulders.

Puffin sat down after she left and watched his television. It was a broadcast from Earth about Tempest, Knight Commander of the Royal Guard. However as soon as he heard Tempest's voice, he realized.

Tempest was the voice in his head.

"It's about time you figured it out." The voice in his head said in a menacing tone. "Now if you tell anyone, I'll kill you where you stand."

With that, Puffin was hiding another secret from the world.

Chapter 39

The egg shook and moved every few minutes. Crow was certain that it could hatch at any moment. But after three weeks of a constant shaking in his pocket, he had resigned himself to ignoring it once again.

Kiva on the other hand, was very excited for the Dragon that was going to hatch from it.

The couple had set up their schedules so that they had their weeks off at the same time. While they were off, they stayed on Earth in Crow's apartment, in the town surrounding the castle.

"I think the day is today." Kiva said, snatching the egg from Crow's hand.

"Why don't you just ask Mirai." Crow said, taking the egg back.

Kiva grabbed the egg back while kissing Crow on the cheek.

Crow smiled.

They had been debating whether or not Dragons imprinted on the first person they saw. Kiva argued that they most certainly did because they hatched from eggs. Crow didn't necessarily believe this because Magical Beasts weren't like regular animals. He still played along.

"So, what will you name it?" Kiva asked.

"I don't know do you have any ideas?"

"How about Maat, after the goddess of truth?"

"No," Crow said, "Numcustos would despise that"

"Okay, how about Prometheus," Kiva attempted, "After the titan that granted mankind fire."

"No." Crow said, "He was doomed to eternal punishment."

"How about Kirby?" Kiva asked.

"Who's Kirby?"

"The greatest of all warriors!" Kiva shouted as she snatched the egg and ran away to the bedroom.

Crow chased after her. The pair laughed and embraced as Crow stole the egg back. They stood for a moment and stared into each other's eyes. Crow noticed that Kiva's magic seal was a different shape than his own.

"I love you." Crow said.

"I love you too." Kiva replied.

It was the first time they'd ever said it out loud to one another. Crow's heart was fluttering with a joy he could not describe. He stared Kiva in the eyes as he smiled. They leaned in to kiss each other.

It was at that exact moment that egg hatched.

It started as a single crack. Before a small silver blur burst through the top of the egg and darted around the room. It bumped into a vase of flowers and they instantly wilted. Then it crashed into an old pillow on the bed, causing it to restore to perfect condition.

"Kiva." Crow said, "Don't touch it."

Crow summoned a Dummy and ordered it to capture the hatchling. The Dummy jumped on top of the bed, swung around the ceiling fan, and tackled the hatchling out of the air. The Dummy's hands turned to straw pieces.

"Your Dummies are made of straw, aren't they?" Kiva said as she sent a small, teal, golem after the hatchling.

The hatchling landed on the Golem, causing the stone monster to turn to dust.

"Numcustos Bestia!"

A magical door opened. Numcustos walked through it wearing a black suit with a derby hat.

"Oh, the egg hatched," Numcustos said.

The Demidemon walked back through into door and re-emerged a few seconds later holding chains and a shiny, purple heart stone for a Golem. He placed the heart stone in the last link of the chain. The heart stone sprouted purple tendrils that connected themselves to the chain.

"I present to you, The Living Chain." Numcustos said, "Crow, you can control it like any other Golem. It doesn't eat. It doesn't sleep. And because it's made from metal found only in Gehenna, it's unbreakable and won't have that instant aging fiasco you're dealing with. It will hold you forever like an ex-lover."

Crow reached out to the Living Chain, and to his surprise it floated into his hand. He felt some of his own energy get sapped into the chain. The chain tripled in length nearly instantly.

The Dragon darted by again, but this time was snagged down to the floor in midair by the chain. The chain proceeded to wrap itself around the dragon.

"I told you it works!"

"Unhand me Demonkin, Elfkin, and I don't know what kin you are." The Dragon shouted in a voice that Crow could only describe as, "adorable."

"No." Numcustos Bestia said, "You made a mess of this place. If any Magical Creature is going to make a mess of Crow's apartment, it's me."

"I swear when I learn to breathe fire, I'll burn you up."

"I'm from Gehenna baby." Numcustos said, "I bathed in flames before I came here."

"Then I'll age you and everyone in here."

Numcustos Bestia pointed around Crow, "half-elf." Then he pointed at Kiva, "Planet's equivalent to an elf." Finally, he pointed to himself, "demonkin."

"Your point?"

"Everyone here will look young and beautiful forever, the most damage you'd do would be making Crow taller and turning our clothes to dust." Numcustos said, "And I've seen enough naked bodies that that wouldn't phase me."

Crow was annoyed with Numcustos, but he realized that he needed him to help deal with the baby dragon.

"Do you realize that I am an all-powerful Thousand Years Dragon." The baby Dragon said.

Then it burped and started crying.

"That's enough boys." Kiva said as she lifted the Dragon up into her arms. "If you promise not to age anything else, we can take the chains off of you. The Baby Dragon nodded pathetically.

Crow took off the chains. They opened a small magical door and went through.

"Crow, I suggest summoning those once in a while, they're like the 1000 Hands of the Needy."

"What do you mean?"

"There were 1000 hands when you first learned the spell a few years ago. Now you're closer to 5000 hands because they absorb magic from my magical plane. If you didn't use the spell for a year there'd, be 10,000 or more that you couldn't control. Using certain spells keeps them in check while they gradually grow. That chain held onto you for a minute and tripled in length. I just don't want it to be uncontrollable one day. That being said using spells frequently makes them stronger too but more controllable. Your own magic is vast and powerful. I'd think you were a demon if I weren't so aware.

"Is there anything else I should know?"

"Yesterday, Timmy played nice and let us have a snowball fight."

"Good to know." Crow said before turning his attention back to the Baby Dragon.

"Are you hungry?"

"Yes."

"What do you eat?"

"I don't know."

Kiva offered it a piece of candy. The Dragon chewed it, then spat it out. Kiva laughed in a way that betrayed what Crow knew to be anger.

"Let's start with something simpler," Crow said, "what's your name?"

"Name?" The Dragon said.

"What should we call you?" Numcustos said.

"I don't know." The Dragon said.

Numcustos lifted the Dragon by its tail and examined it, "Are you a male or female?"

"Isn't it obvious?" The Dragon said.

"Not at all." Kiva said.

"Which one means boy?"

"Male." Crow answered.

"I'm a male."

"That's good.

"Numcustos, do Dragons have typical names?"

"Of course they do." Numcustos said, "they're all Ladon. Ladon this, Ladon that. Ladon who cares."

"My name is Ladon Chronosimi!" The Dragon shouted before fluttering around the room.

154

"Welcome aboard Ladon Chronosimi." Crow said, "You learned to talk fast."

"I know bits and pieces of things I'm going to learn." Simi replied, sitting back on his hind legs like a dog at attention.

"Well, that's convenient." Crow said, "What's something I can do to keep you happy?"

"I want to grow powerful."

"Then stick with us kid." Numcustos said.

"Nice to meet you, Simi." Kiva said.

Chapter 40

Raven stood at attention. Beside him was Crow. In front of them, also at attention were Easter, Tempest, and Tornado. Staring down at them from his golden throne was The Drakon King.

The king's usually immaculate hair was a mess. His beard was overgrown. He had bags under his eyes. For a man that quite literally had all the time he needed to rest and rejuvenate himself, The Drakon King seemed exhausted.

"Do you have any idea why you're all in here?"

"No, your majesty." The Royal Knights said in unison.

"You're here because I woke up and we still knew next to nothing about The Beast Knights or their leader, The Chimera King. So, I stopped time for the Milky Way and went for a walk."

"Sire!" Easter shouted, "The entire Milky Way. That's a lot, even for you."

"I'm aware." The Drakon King said, slightly raising his voice.

"Forgive me your majesty."

"There's nothing to forgive," The Drakon King said, "In all honesty I have no idea how long it was frozen for. Long enough for me to explore the whole of the area and so I found something notable. I guess as long or short a time as I needed. Time travel is complicated."

A large cage was carted into the room by a pair of Martians in Knight armor. It contained a large grey alien with red eyes and long white hair running down his back. It was sitting, unmoving as if it were waiting for something. It was clearly a Beast Knight.

None of the Royal Guards flinched.

"Your Majesty, is he frozen in time?" Easter said.

"No." The Drakon King answered, "But he is in a cage that has been graded to hold a Gehenna Beast."

"There are things way stronger than Gehenna Beasts, Your Majesty." Crow said.

"I'm aware." The Drakon King said.

Suddenly the Beast Knight sprung to life. Raven instinctually grabbed the hilt of his Dark Star Blade while the alien began thrashing in the cage.

"Chimera King!" The Beast Knight bellowed. "I... Sorry... Chimera King."

"Silence!" Tempest shouted, "You insolent beast, you are in the presence of The Drakon King, the one true King."

"Chimera King!" The Beast Knight shouted, "Save me. I... Captured..."

The Beast Knight continued thrashing until the cage walls broke revealing that he had been behind some sort of magic barrier as well that flashed blue as soon as soon as the Beast Knight made contact. The Beast Knight punched at the barrier until it became visible.

The Royal Guards were all now armed and prepared to attack. Raven's blade glowed a dark red color, Crow had summoned Numcustos Bestia and a small Dragon to his side. Easter had made chains from the orbs that were floating in front of her. Tornado drew a Blood Star hilted Beam Sword.

Raven glanced at Tornado and questioned how a non-Mage could obtain such a weapon. Tornado was the most mysterious of the Royal Guard. He never spoke of his experiences or past battles like the others, he refused apprentices, and he only seemed to create more questions the more Raven learned about him.

"Kill... Dragon.... King." The alien shouted as it punched the barrier.

Before any of them could act, Tempest killed the Beast Knight. It had to have been Tempest. He was the only one that moved. He lifted his hand and the Beast Knight's neck snapped as he collapsed to the ground.

"Tempest!" Easter shouted, "You didn't need to kill him!"

She broke position, marched up to Tempest and poked him in the chest.

Tempest in turn sneered down at the half-elf and said, "he posed a threat to The Drakon King whom we are sworn to protect. I could have captured him but he'd have gotten free eventually."

Usually this would have seen the two senior knights engage in a heated argument. However, in front of The Drakon King, they wouldn't dare. Much like Crow and Raven's squabbles, Tempest and Easter more often than not found themselves diametrically opposed.

"Regardless of why Tempest killed it, it's dead now." The Drakon King said, "Crow and Raven, you're out on recon. Easter and Tornado you're with me."

"And me, your majesty."

"Tempest, you're going to dispose of the corpse that you so graciously left in my hall."

"I imagine you knew what was going to happen."

"I had an inkling."

Chapter 41

Five minutes before The Drakon King captured the Beast Knight, Silverback was walking around a pier at sunset in a rare moment of peace without Kuma, Mink, or Lioness.

Peace was a funny word for Silverback. His job required him to desecrate corpses, sometimes kill. All in the servitude of his unseen master, The Drakon King. Even on hubworlds where alien life forms of all shapes and sizes converged, Silverback was an anomaly. Gray skin was uncommon in the Milky Way. Especially on planets without a history of magic.

Silverback wasn't sure why he was walking. He just knew that he was told to Get as far away from the children without causing a commotion as he possibly could. So Silverback took off in broad daylight. He even left his precious eyeballs in a bag neatly tucked in to his pillow.

The pier creaked beneath each step Silverback took. To his left a wave crashed into the side of the pier lightly blowing a cool mist onto Silverback's face.

And then, everything froze.

Silverback didn't blink. He didn't move. He was in shock behind a magical barrier and an iron cage. The iron was purely in case he was a product of necromancy. Though, it didn't seem he was. He'd often wondered whether Beast Knights were undead, despite constant assurances to the contrary, he avoided iron and silver, just in case. Though he was in an iron cage, not burning.

Silverback calmed down enough to recognize his surroundings. Directly in front of him was the warm, calming presence of his master, The Chimera King. The Chimera King was as beautiful as he'd remembered. He was a tall, slender man with golden brown skin, pointed ears, and piercing brown eyes. The Chimera King was dressed in an ornate set of jade armor with a purple cape. Holstered you're his hip was a beam pistol. The Chimera King was standing in a group of people, each wearing similar armor and weapons.

"Chimera King!" The Beast Knight bellowed as he thrashed against the cage, "I... Sorry... Chimera King."

"Silence!" The Chimera King shouted, "You insolent beast, you are in the presence of The Drakon King, the one true King."

"Chimera King!" Silverback struggled to shout, "Save me. I... Captured..."

The Beast Knight continued thrashing until the cage walls broke revealing that he had been behind some sort of magic barrier as well that flashed blue as soon as soon as the Beast Knight made contact. The Beast Knight punched at the barrier until it became visible.

The Royal Guards were all now armed and prepared to attack. A knight's blade glowed a light-yellow color. Silverback started thinking about ways to break a beam sword. He would need to break the Knight's wrist and then break the hilt of their blade.

Another Knight had summoned a small demon and a small Dragon to his side. Silverback admittedly had no idea how he would neutralize monsters.

A third Knight had made chains from the floor tiles that were floating in front of her. Silverback started to realize that alone, he couldn't take four full-fledged knights at one time. He would need to take out the most important target. This would be a suicide mission. He needed to protect The Chimera King.

An older Knight drew a Blood Star sword. Being killed by that would cause Silverback's soul to be bound. He wasn't sure he could survive that. He wasn't sure that he still had a soul, but he wasn't happy to risk it.

Silverback scanned the room for any remaining targets. That was when he saw the bearded man with shining gold armor. The purpose of his existence. Silverback was staring at The Drakon King. His plan suddenly changed, if he could free himself, all he would need was three seconds to break The Drakon King's neck. He could grab him with his hands or use some other part of his concealed physiology to do it.

"Kill... Dragon.... King." The Beast Knight shouted as he punched the barrier. He made sure he was loud enough to be heard by The Chimera King.

Then everything went black again.

160

When Silverback awoke, he was in a morgue. He could tell before he opened his eyes. He knew the smells. He knew the sounds of the fluorescent lights. He knew the buzz of magic used to preserve corpses as it tinged his skin. It was a familiar scene. He had died again, only to be brought back to life. He sat up on the cold steel table. Standing at his feet was The Chimera King.

"I... Sorry... Chimera King." Silverback managed to stammer out.

"Silverback," The Chimera King said outloud, "You have nothing to apologize for."

"I... failed..." Silverback said.

"It's not your fault." The Chimera King said, "If anything, this just highlights the evils of the Flock. You all have been looking after yourselves for far too long. I shall send all of my Beast Knights coordinates in the coming days. It's time that I officially took control of my kingdom."

The Chimera King placed his hand on Silverback's chest and suddenly Silverback was back on the pier where he'd been before this adventure started. At his feet was small pile of dead rodents.

He stared at the horizon, smiling brightly. He had met The Chimera King. He felt loved. Silverback began to walk back toward his hideout when he noticed another Beast Knight suddenly appear on the hub world standing on a pile of rodents. Then another. Then ten more. Then another larger group. Soon the entire pier was full of Beast Knights.

The people on the pier and in the surrounding area began panicking. The commotion was loud and disorganized. And then it was quickly nothing. A common thought passed through the Beast Knights, a message from their master, "destroy machines and kill everyone who isn't one of us."

More Beast Knights appeared every few seconds. The Hubworld citizens didn't stand a chance. Eventually the Beast Knights had filled every street, ran into every building, and brutally killed every living being on the hubworld. To Silverback,

"How good is it for our family to finally all be together." The Chimera King said as he appeared atop a building. He was using some sort of magic to make his voice louder. The Beast Knights howled and cheered in response. Silverback joined them.

Chapter 42

Puffin was waist deep in water. He was vomiting uncontrollably. The whole time thinking, he'd magically teleported to an apparent artificial planet. He counted the laws he'd broken; potential necromancy, using magic in a hubworld, accessory to homicide, and human teleportation. If he was discovered, he could potentially spend the rest of his life in a prison.

Dead rats floated past him, the product of teleportation. Further in the water, a blue skinned corpse began sinking beneath the surface. He wanted to at least rescue the body but every fiber in his body was telling him not to save it.

It smelled of carnage. Puffin was unsure how the Beast Knights managed to continue in these conditions. They were a crowd. They were an ocean of blood thirsty monsters. Puffin was disgusted. Still though a part of him was elated to be there.

"How good it is to have my family here." The voice of The Chimera King rang all over the hubworld and inside Puffin's mind.

"By now the rest of the Kingdom of the Flock knows this so I'll make it clear, I am The Chimera King. I am the true King of all known space and time." The Chimera King said as he paced back and forth, "Everyone here has literally died for The Drakon Kingdom. Your ships were not maintained and exploded. You were sent on the front lines of planetary conquest and never made it home to your families. You weren't properly educated about magic and suffered the results. You were punished for violating laws that weren't fair to your circumstances."

The crowd of Beast Knights booed and hissed.

"You died." The Chimera King yelled, "You died and I brought you back to life as my knights. Do not worry, this is not necromancy, this is perfect reincarnation. A power long since lost to us. A power that magic itself feels only I am worthy of. You have been reincarnated and once I've reached my goals, you will all be free to pursue your own."

Puffin stopped paying attention to The Chimera King as he began formulating a plan. He started running to the beach, shoving every Beast Knight that wouldn't move out of the way. Out of breath and shaking, Puffin began drawing the runes to open a magic door in the sand. As soon as the door opened, Puffin could see that it wouldn't be large enough. He panicked silently. That's when he disappeared.

"I can read your mind, I know you wanted to tell your Captain." The Chimera King said inside his head, "it doesn't matter, The Beast Kingdom, your true kingdom is unstoppable."

Chapter 43

Crow was in shock. He'd known his father was morally corrupt, but knowing that Tempest was The Chimera King was a complete surprise. He was going to be questioned.

"I'm just going to surrender myself." Crow said after a day of thinking.

"No, you are not." Numcustos Bestia replied.

"Why not?" Chronosimi asked, "if Crow did nothing wrong, then they'll let him go."

"Look kid, you're new here," Numcustos said as he put an arm around Simi's neck, "They're still going to want to interrogate him. Humans, elves, dwarves, and orc kin are all pretty terrible. They say innocent until proven guilty. But it's the other way around."

"I don't believe that." Chronosimi said. The Dragon's eyes widened like a hungry kitten as he turned his gaze from Crow to Numcustos Bestia and back several times.

"What does Kiva think about your stupid idea?" Numcustos Bestia asked.

"Smart idea." Chronosimi said.

"She can't get involved because of her position as Mirai's guard."

Before anyone could respond a rapping at the door interrupted the conversation.

"Crow. We know you're in there." The voice was Owl.

"I told you they were going to come for you." Numcustos whispered.

"The last I checked," Crow said, "I did nothing wrong."

"You're a suspect in an attempted coup." Owl's voice broke and was replaced by the deep voiced groan of an Orc. They were trying to lure Crow out.

He was forced to choose between a peaceful escape or property destruction.

Crow stood up and unlocked his door. He paused briefly letting three Orcs into his apartment.

"Hands where I can see them," the largest orc said, "don't try any of that magic business."

Crow raised his hands. Behind him, Numcustos Bestia and Chronosimi also assumed the same position.

The smallest orc of the group lumbered over to Crow and lifted the half-elf over his shoulder.

"Come on." Crow groaned, "you didn't need to lift me up like that. I'm not a runner."

"No." The orc said, "but you are a mage and I'm not taking any chances."

Crow groaned. "If I wanted to escape with magic, I could do it while you're lifting me up. I don't use magic books or a wand or a staff. My two familiars here could also pull me into another dimension. I am leaving here with you of my own free will."

The orc stopped walking and threw Crow violently onto the floor in a slight panic.

"You could most certainly have put me down nicely."

"Come with us or I'll break your spine." The largest orc bellowed.

"I was already coming with you!" Crow shouted.

They walked from the apartment building to a large black car parked across the street. Thunder rumbled in the sky as Crow was pushed into the car and seated between two snarling Orcs. The third orc, the one that had been carrying him was driving. Numcustos Bestia and Chronosimi shared the passenger seat. The smell inside the car could only be described as ghastly. Crow wanted to vomit.

Crow felt annoyed as a sharp elbow jabbed into his ribs. He was now painfully aware of how useless his would-be captors were. These were new Knights. In his year as a full-fledged Knight, Crow had grown to understand that if he were truly wanted they would have sent experienced Knights. Specifically, they would have either sent mages or Knights with some capability of Anti Magic. Though the latter was incredibly rare even amongst the most experienced Knights.

Hours later, Crow was in a holding cell. He assumed he was in the castle.

He attempted to use magic to transform the space into something more comfortable. The attempt was futile, instead, Crow was stuck alone in a cold, wet, cement room with only a bench, a table, a chess board and two wooden chairs to keep him company. He imagined that he would be interrogated by a high-ranking knight, perhaps Easter or Goose. In times like these, Knights of the Flock were trained to focus on something to keep panic from settling in. Crow generally thought this was a useless exercise and never practiced it, but he still went back to his training and counted individual seconds. After an hour, nobody appeared.

Crow sat down on a metal bench. He began to notice water dripping from the ceiling. The water brought the comfort of knowing he probably wasn't frozen in time. He tried calling Numcustos Bestia and Chronosimi, while he could feel their presence neither appeared.

After another hour he decided to lie on the bench and stare at the ceiling. The leak stopped on its own but there was now a clear wet patch where it had been. Crow wondered what had caused the leak. He lost track of time.

The lights shut off outside the room. Crow wondered if he would be there overnight. Then the door opened. What walked in was a Garuda. The Garuda were an alien species of bipeds that had evolved from their planet's birds. This one was small. It's head and beak looked rigid as if they had been through a lifetime of battles. It's brilliant red and orange feathers were covered mostly by a suit of light armor that covered its torso and legs but left its wings which ended in hook shaped, talon-like hands open. Crow imagined the armor was more for modesty than for functionality as Garuda feathers and eggs were used to make buildings on their home planet, Rakim.

The Garuda glared down at Crow without blinking for what felt like minutes. Crow wasn't sure what he was supposed to feel, he didn't feel nervous but he didn't feel Relaxed either.

"Are you a Beast Knight?" Asked the Garuda, at least Crow thought. Crow was certain the Garuda spoke, but it didn't move in the slightest. Instead, the sound was made by some sort of digital speaker attached to its armor.

"No." Crow replied.

"Do you worship the god, Bodur?" The Garuda asked.

Crow had never heard of the god Bodur, "I'm an agnostic."

"Do you eat meat?" The Garuda asked.

"Yes." Crow replied, "What does that have to do with anything?"

"What's your favorite color?"

Crow sighed, "Purple."

"When is the last time you communicated with your father?"

"I was in a meeting with him a few weeks ago." Crow answered, "He killed a Beast Knight."

"Do you believe The Drakon King deserves to die?" The Garuda asked.

"No."

The Garuda blinked then resumed their intense stare.

"Have you traveled outside of the Milky Way?"

Crow was bewildered by the question, it was literally his job."Yes."

"Are you a Beast Knight?"

Crow answered plainly, "No."

"Do you eat candy?"

"Only chocolate." Crow answered.

"Are you a Beast Knight?"

"Are you a moron?" Crow replied.

"No." The Garuda said while tilting their head, "Do you support The Drakon King."

"Yes."

"Where is your father?" The Garuda asked. It then pecked at bug flying around the prison cell and ate it while Crow responded.

"I said I don't know."

"Where is Tempest?"

"I don't know."

"Where are your siblings?"

"I really don't know that one. We don't talk." Crow laughed.

"You have hundreds of siblings." The Garuda said as they tilted their head, "you don't know any of their locations?"

"Absolutely not." Crow's voice got slightly louder.

"Are you a Beast Knight?"

Time froze. The Garuda was caught mid-blink. Crow could still move freely, which meant that The Drakon King would be walking through the door.

As The Drakon King entered the room he looked visibly haggard. His normally immaculate hair and beard were unkempt. His eyes had dark circles under them. His clothing was wrinkled. It was as if he hadn't slept in weeks.

"Sir, are you okay?" Crow asked immediately.

"Yes." The Drakon King replied, "I've exhausted my magical abilities lately. Some of the spells I use to refresh myself aren't quite packing any punch."

Crow understood this all to well. He personally hadn't cleaned his apartments in years. Instead, he'd used magic to change the space into a cleaner area. When he first learned to summon 1000 Hands of the Needy, he couldn't manage this and had to learn how to make his own bed.

"So can I leave now?" Crow asked.

"You're not free." The Drakon King said.

"I'm assuming the conversation is one that the Garuda can't hear."

"That would be correct"

"Well, I don't know where any one in my family is." Crow said petulantly.

"That's not what I want to know." The Drakon King said, "I want to know what you know about your magical attributes."

"I'm surrounded by a plain of Gehenna. It enables me to summon creatures and objects at will. But that was in my file."

The Drakon King frowned, "So you don't know."

"Know what?" Crow said.

"It's easier if I show you."

The Drakon King placed his hand on Crow's face. Then everything went white.

Chapter 44

Crow had no idea where he was. He was standing beside The Drakon King in an open blue space. There wasn't a true ceiling or a floor as everything seemed to blend into itself. It was as if they were standing inside a bubble surrounded by water.

"This is the Void, or the as you may know it the area beyond space and time." The Drakon King said, "It is the well from which all Time Magic derives."

"There's nothing here." Crow said, looking around.

"There is everything and nothing here. Everything that ever will exist, everything that has existed."

"So do you have your own plane of The Void?"

"Absolutely not." The Drakon King replied as he stroked his beard. "There's no plane to be had."

"Why are we here?" Crow asked, "How are we here?"

Hundreds of gilded thrones appeared from thin air around the pair. Each throne was occupied by a gigantic magical beast with a gold seal surrounding their left eye. Crow was not familiar with what any of the creatures were.

"You are in the theatre of kings." The Drakon King said, "these are the Avatars."

"Avatars of what?"

"The Avatars of the magical realms. The creators of all magic."

An Avatar that was at least twenty feet tall, made of blue flames somewhat resembling a Flame Nought grasped as the hand rests of his throne. Beside him a gigantic suit of armor, that must have been an Avatar, moved in its throne.

Crow couldn't feel the magic emanating from the kings but it was clearly radiating from them. A small patch of grass formed around an Avatar that Crow could only describe as a man shaped oak tree. Clouds formed over the head of an Avatar that looked to be a gigantic Water Nought. Each strange occurrence contained to the area immediately surrounding the associated Avatar.

A wisp of smoke appeared in the middle of the circle next to Crow and The Drakon King. From the smoke, an elven man wearing a purple robe emerged. The man also bore a gold crest on his left eye, though he had a much less happy disposition than The Drakon King.

Crow stared, "Who's that?"

"The Wyrm King, several kings before me." The Drakon King said, "Long ago, he stormed into the Court of Magic and demanded his own throne. This is what occurred."

Suddenly the still figures of the Avatars all sprang to life. Crow was able to hear, smell, and feel all of their presence.

"And whom are you?" The Avatar of Flame Magic said in a voice that sounded as threatening as he appeared.

"They call me the Wyrm King, the King of Man, the King of Elves, the King of Dwarves and the King of Orcs."

"So, you're Avatar of the pathetic beings on your pathetic planet." The Avatar of Water Magic said.

"I believe I am the rightful King of all of you."

Laughter erupted in the room. A giant Avatar made of bricks stood up from his throne three rows back, walked to the Wyrm King and picked up the elf in his gigantic hand.

"You do have a Gold Seal." The Avatar made of bricks said, "But it means nothing."

"What do you mean?" The Wyrm King asked in a frustrated tone.

"Your realm. The realm of mortals, has no magic."

"Yes, it does." The Wyrm King said defiantly.

"No." The Avatar made of bricks said, "your universe picks up the excess magic of all of ours."

"Yes."

"And without an activated seal, your people can never fully utilize their magic."

"That is why I am here. To have my seal activated and assume my place on a throne."

Again, the hall erupted into laughter.

A human sized Avatar enshrouded by a black cloak walked to the center of the circle in front of the Wyrm King. It had a normal gait, no visible inhuman traits, and made no discernible magical traces. Crow was convinced he was looking at another person from their universe.

"Who's this guy?" Crow asked.

"Bodur, The Avatar of Death Magic." The Drakon King explained, "At this point in time he was the most powerful Avatar."

Bodur was someone The Garuda had asked Crow about during the interrogation.

"It would seem that you truly believe that you wish to rule that which you do not understand." Bodur said. He had an unusual way of speaking, stretching out each vowel while speaking at a tone just above a whisper. "I do not believe that you have the right to claim such things."

Bodur placed a hand that on the Wyrm King's chest. Crow could feel a chill suddenly grip the room. It was the first thing he'd actually felt the entire time he was there.

The Wyrm King immediately pushed the Avatar of Death's hand away revealing it to be a clean skeletal hand adorned with magical runes that had been carved onto each bone.

"I am not to be touched."

"Believe me. Nobody shall ever touch you again." Bodur said. "As long as you live."

Crow could hear the smile in the Avatar's voice.

The void emptied itself leaving only Crow, The Drakon King, and the Wyrm King.

Immediately a throne room sprang up around them. It was not unlike The Drakon King's though the artwork was more contemporary with the Gothic era. A large stone statue of a gargoyle overlooked the throne. Crow wondered if was a real gargoyle as they were notoriously difficult to tame, especially the breeds that could turn to stone.

The Wyrm King appeared confused. All of the royal servants stopped in their tracks to attend to their suddenly appeared monarch. He opened his mouth as if to say something. No words escaped his lips as he dropped to the ground dead.

Pieces of paper floated to the floor of the castle as if they were snowflakes. Crow caught one and read it.

"The King has died."

Use of teleportation shall kill you too.

Tomorrow someone will awaken with a gold seal on their eye. More will awaken with blue seals.

We have granted you magical abilities.

The gold seal shall be your new king."

Crow looked around and everything was stopped.

"What happened next?" Crow asked.

"They planned a search for the new king. But he was luckily a much more liked Lord from a rival family."

"Then our magic comes from the Avatars?"

"Not quite." The Drakon King said as he pointed to the gold seal on his eye. "It comes from the King's seal. An activated gold seal allows for the existence of magic in a realm. Our realm doesn't have a specific magic type, but as long as this seal is active, mages can exist without being personally gifted Magic. At the same time, the Avatars exist because of us. Whenever a concept is created in our realm, a magic is created and so is an Avatar. One cannot exist without the other."

"What does any of this have to do with why I'm in this cell?" Crow said, finally frustrated with his present situation. The Void faded around them and the cell came back into place. The Garuda still hadn't completed his blink yet.

"I believe Tempest has a gold seal."

"Wouldn't that mean you both were king then?" Crow asked. It wasn't that he was confused, it was that the concept of there being two kings went against everything he knew up until this moment.

"It would mean that this war is just beginning."

Chapter 45

Raven stared in disbelief at Kiva and Mirai, "I'm not doing that."

"Why not?" Mirai said.

"Because, The Flock is in a war, I should be fighting. Not babysitting." Raven said. He wasn't sure why, but the annoyance in his voice made him feel like Crow.

"Hey!" Mirai shouted, "I am the Regent of this planet. I'm also one of two known users of Time Magic in the entire universe. You are not babysitting. You are guarding perhaps the most special person that ever existed."

Raven frowned. Mirai smiled. Raven silently admitted defeat by shrugging his shoulders.

They were back on Aesop. Though Raven was not at first happy with the assignment, it was a relief that he was not one of the Knights being questioned for treason.

"So, as I was saying before I was so rudely denied my ability to explain," Mirai said as she stared Raven in the eye. "We're going to the surface to search for The Black Orb."

"What's a Black Orb?" Raven asked.

"It's a magical item needed to summon a Cinder Bird." Kiva said.

"Absolutely not."

"When did you turn into such a chicken?" Mirai said.

"What did you say?"

"You heard me." Mirai said, "Ever since you got your ass kicked at the Test of Strength you've been a chicken. We need a Cinder Bird! I had a lot of visions. A Phoenix saves the kingdom. We need the Phoenix. We need it! If the Phoenix doesn't rise, bad things happen."

"I have not been a chicken." Raven said through gritted teeth, "I've been studying strategy."

"Then put that sword of yours to use." Mirai said.

Mirai marched out of the room as she clucked like a chicken. Kiva followed. Raven sat and thought. He questioned whether Mirai was right or not. He had moved so far from rushing headfirst into every situation to thinking so intensely and slowly that he cost real lives.

"Fine." Raven said.

Mirai turned around. "If you're even the slightest bit unsure, I'll request another Knight to accompany me."

Raven walked up to Mirai so her eyes were level with his chest. "I'm sure."

"Good."

A few hours later they were walking on the surface of Aesop. At least Raven and Kiva were walking. Mirai had made Kiva summon a golem to carry the Regent.

The surface of Aesop was a true wasteland. There was nothing except dry cracked ground. All life on Aesop was underground, including the plants. The surface was essentially the largest empty parking lot Raven had ever seen. He smiled at the thought of thousands of ships landing in perfectly aligned rows.

"Crow told me you're studying under his father." Kiva said.

"Yeah." Raven said, "not anymore."

"Did you have any idea?" Kiva said.

"Absolutely not." Raven said.

"Do you know where Crow is?" Kiva said, "I haven't heard from him in days."

"Kiva," Raven said, "You know I can't discuss Knights of the Flock business."

"That's a lie and you know it."

"It's not a lie." Raven said as he tripped over a golem's footprint.

The heat began to make Raven feel like he could melt. Mirai and the golem were far ahead of them.

"Do you know where we're going?"

"We're not going anywhere specific." Kiva answered. "The Black Orb appears for people that deserve it. On the surface of Aesop."

Raven was beginning to doubt in the wisdom behind their quest.

"But I know it's going to appear today." Mirai shouted back..

"So why are we looking for it?" Raven asked, surprised that it had taken him that long to ask why they were walking around a wasteland.

"A Cinder Bird will eventually turn into a Phoenix. A Phoenix can use its fires to heal any affliction. Some have said it can even change Knights back into regular people."

"So, you're saying if we find the Black Orb we can use it to control a Cinder Bird and end the war."

Suddenly a shadow eclipsed the sun. Raven was momentarily relieved by a break in the sun, but was immediately horrified when he saw the giant black figure of a bird with impossibly long tail feathers. Raven didn't know the words to describe the size of this magical beast. Its head was larger than most buildings in the underground city. Its wings were as wide as a city block. The only way it could possibly have flown was through magic. Its very existence defied physics. Just bringing it down would cause a crater that would resemble a bomb impact.

"There is no way that we bring that thing down."

"We're going to have it land peacefully." Kiva said.

Kiva reached down into her bag and pulled out a handful of papers with magical runes scrawled on them. "Crow gave me some summoning tags in case of emergency." She threw the tag onto the dry, cracked ground. The piece of paper immediately burst into flames and danced around until a magical door appeared from the ground.

Raven was disappointed when the only thing that emerged was Numcustos Bestia. The Demidemon was wearing a suit pants, an undershirt, and sunglasses.

Raven wondered why Numcustos wasn't wearing his usual three-piece suit.

"For what reason have I been summoned?" Numcustos said. He sounded unenthused, as if he were being forced.

"Numcustos Bestia, I need you to help us capture that Cinder Bird and place it in Crow's Plane of Gehenna." Kiva said as she pointed to the

"As you..." Numcustos started before he shook his head, "As you can clearly see that thing in the sky is what we in the biz call an adult male Cinder Bird. It's probably about to molt into a Phoenix. No offense but none of you are equipped for this. There's no way to hold it. Because it's trans dimensional."

"Trans what?" Raven said.

"Oh, you beautiful fool." Numcustos said, "You know Kiva, brains wise I get why you like Crow. But as far as human specimens go, Raven definitely is the pick of the litter. Anyway, the bird can switch between multiple magical planes. It can go to Gehenna, Earth, Ignis, or Elysia. Basically, if it is a plane of Fire, Life, Beasts, or Death the Cinder Bird can go there. I can't contain it even in Crow's plane of Gehenna because it can freely travel to other dimensions without being summoned. But. You already knew that didn't you."

Numcustos Bestia turned to Mirai who was pretending not to listen to the Demidemon.

Raven was confused by what was happening. The little Demidemon jumped up and down in anger as he cursed Mirai's name. Mirai whom was only a head taller than Numcustos Bestia tried to ignore him, then she attempted to pacify him. Finally, Mirai gave up and slapped Numcustos across the face. Numcustos lunged at the Regent. Before he could reach her, Raven grabbed the Demidemon out of the air.

"Would someone please explain what is going on." Raven said as Numcustos Bestia bit his hand.

"I have nothing to do with this." Kiva said.

"The Regent had me summoned here so that Crow could be left on Earth. Because something bad is going to happen."

"Mirai," Kiva shouted, "Is this true."

Mirai didn't answer.

"Crow needs Numcustos Bestia to summon anything bigger than he is. Did you leave him there on purpose?"

Again, Mirai didn't answer.

"Just explain yourself Mirai." Raven said.

Kiva was visibly struggling to hold back tears. She began pacing back and forth before marching directly into Mirai.

"I'm saving Aesop." Mirai whimpered, "first I thought if we could capture the Cinderbird we'd have a chance against the Beast Knights. Then I thought, if we had Numcustos Bestia, we could summon the leviathan he has hidden."

"I do not have a leviathan." Numcustos started.

"I know you do. I've seen your future."

"Well, I don't have one." Numcustos said, "It's my great white whale."

"Why wouldn't you bring Crow with him?"

"Oh yeah." Numcustos said, "Crow is in jail on Earth."

"Numcustos Bestia, tell me everything that is happening or so help me, I'll pluck every hair off your furry little body, use them to stuff a golem, and beat you with it for the rest of eternity." Kiva shouted.

Numcustos ran and hid behind Raven.

"You being with Crow makes way more sense now." Numcustos said. Raven groaned.

Numcustos told them everything about how Crow had turned himself in and was now being held captive. He also expressed that he was unsure how but he was for the time being, acting independent of Crow.

Raven looked up in the sky to see the Cinder Bird flying away. In a way, he was relieved. He did not want to try and fight that beast of a fowl.

"Numcustos, open a door." Kiva ordered.

"To where?"

"To Earth." Mirai is going to use her diplomatic immunity to fix all of these problems.

"Fine. But I'm going to warn you, this won't be pleasant like the last time Raven here traveled through Gehenna. The only good thing is you'll be able to exit as fast as you enter."

Numcustos opened the door. On the other side, Raven could see what looked like a holding cell. He tried to reach through the door and felt a burning sensation then radiated from his fingertips to the rest of his body.

"Why does it hurt." Raven asked as he pulled his hand back.

"My magic is attuned specifically for Demons." Numcustos said as he walked through the door, "If you travel through my portal with Crow it will hurt."

Every fiber of Raven's being was screaming at him to run through the portal. Every single lesson of his training for had taught him to avoid those instincts.

"I'm going." Raven said, "You guys take a ship to Earth."

He took a step back and readied himself to jump in. Before he could, Kiva lunged herself through the door and it slammed shut behind her.

Chapter 46

Magical doors were inherently designed to function for the being that summoned them in the first place. If a humanoid opened a door and a magical creature went through, the magical creature would go through immense pain. Crow's magical doors to his realm were attuned to both humanoids and the creatures that dwelled there, but only if Crow opened the door. Otherwise, he had no idea the lasting effects of traveling through magical gates. It was for this reason that Crow was not a fan of the Tunneling Method that Knights of the Flock were using to travel great distances by walking through pocket dimensions surrounding mages.

It was for this reason, Crow was just as relieved as he was infuriated when he saw Kiva erupt from a magical door that he hadn't summoned, belonging to Numcustos Bestia. Sulking behind her was Numcustos himself.

"Magic doesn't work here?" Crow asked as Kiva ran up to him and started the tightest embrace of his life.

"It doesn't." Kiva said. "Numcustos wormed his way into the room."

Crow smiled. It felt like the first time in ages.

"Crow." Kiva said as she looked deep into his eyes.

"Yes."

"Are you a follower of The Chimera King?"

"No."

"Are you a follower of Bodur?"

Crow took a step back. He was certain that he had felt a portal open from his plain of Gehenna. He was sure Kiva felt real in his arms.

"When was the last time you spoke to your father?"

"You can stop the simulation." Crow said as he sat down on the bench.

Kiva faded into nothingness as the light around Numcustos refracted away revealing the Garuda. The feathers on the Garuda's face moved around as he grew visibly frustrated.

"Very perceptive." The digital voice of the bird-like creature said.

"You had a major flaw in your projection.

"What was that?"

"Numcustos Bestia was too quiet. He's not a true familiar, he's loud, obnoxious, and rude."

The Garuda made a face, it wasn't a frown because the beak couldn't curl, but it looked disappointed.

"Where is she?"

"I have not been informed."

It was at that moment, the door to the cell opened. A massive Orc-Elf guard in dark green armor walked in. Behind him was the comparatively smaller frame of Raven whom was wearing his civilian clothes, bound at the wrists and ankles.

"In." The Orc-Elf ordered as he tossed Raven into the cell. Raven in turn hit the ground with "thud" that reverberated off the cell walls. The cuffs binding his wrists and ankles beeped and fell to the floor as he stood up.

The Garuda looked at Raven and said, "You were not in my data. I will return shortly."

The two Knights stared at each other for a moment. Crow was equal parts relieved and disappointed to see Raven.

"Prove your real?" Crow said as he collected himself quickly.

"How?"

"What did you order the first time we went out with Mirai and Kiva?"

"Cheese fries." Raven said. A slight smile crossed his lips. "They are a marvel of modern technology."

"It's you alright." Crow said. "So they captured you too?"

"They got me on reentry. I was on Aesop." Raven said, "All the royal guards are being held captive."

Crow's heart sank. Had Kiva been captured? Had the Royal Guards all turned on The Drakon King?

"Kiva's fine. She's with Numcustos Bestia. She dived through a door to come find you." Raven said, "Mirai got special dispensation for faster than light travel. Imagine, between that and tunneling, we could

"So why are we allowed to share a cell?"

"My honest guess is we're low priority. Members of the Gaggle are patrolling the Castle. If we tried to escape, they'd be able to pick us apart. There's a magic dampening field turned on in the castle. Only the most powerful mages like Swan and The Drakon King could use their full abilities here."

This made everything make sense. A magic dampening field would certainly even the playing field in a fight against his father, if his father truly was holding a Gold seal.

"Hey is that a chess board in the corner?"

Crow stared for a second. "How about we play to pass the time."

They sat down. While Crow and Raven weren't fond of one another, they were not opposed to playing with one another after regularly playing games together in their downtime as part of a larger group.

The pieces and board were made of marble. Crow smirked. Even in the dungeons, everything in the Castle was ornate. The two set the board and sat across from one another.

"Pawn to E-4" Crow said as he moved his first piece.

"Pawn to E-5" Raven answered.

"Knight to C-3." Crow said, "How long do you think we're going to be held?"

"Rook to C-5." Raven said, "Until they capture The Chimera King."

"Knight to A-4," Crow said.

"Rook to F-2 and I'm taking you pawn, check."

"That's useless this early in the game." Crow said as he took Raven's Rook with his King.

"Queen to H-4. Check." Raven said, "Hey Crow, remember when Mirai predicted we would fight. Who do you think would win if we fought today?"

"King to E-3." Crow said without hesitation, "I would. You've gotten stronger and you have your Anti-Magic abilities. But you either rush into things or think so much that you suffer. Why is that?"

"Queen to F-4. Check." Raven said, "I don't know that that's true. I think that even without Anti-Magic, I could take you out. You rely too heavily on having others get their hand dirty for you."

"I think you fail to see the big picture. An out and out victory isn't always necessary to achieve a goal." Crow said as he moved his King, "I would never knowingly go into a fight with you, a weapons specialist, without magic at my disposal. King to D-3 by the way. It'd be a fool's errand."

"Pawn to D-5." Raven said, "So you'd run from a fight with me, just like you are now."

"King to C-3." Crow replied, "I'm not running. I'm just redefining victory. I don't let anger or fear or impulse determine my course of action."

"Queen to F4. Queen takes Pawn." Raven said.

"King to B3." Crow said.

The game went on for what felt like hours, though in reality, it had only been a few moments. To Crow the game was reflective of everything he'd learned about Raven. Crow responded by primarily using his King as a both an offensive weapon and a means of escape. Eventually the two found themselves in a place of mutually assured destruction.

"Damnit." Raven said.

"What?" Crow asked.

"If I move to put you in check, you have a relatively easy checkmate."

"So, it's a draw then?"

"Yes." Raven said then immediately stood up and walked away from the chess board. Crow was disappointed. Raven didn't even at least try to play out the game or explain his thought processes.

It was at this moment that the ceiling crashed down into the room. Before Crow could see anything, he felt a warm sensation radiate from his left eye to the rest of his body. Whatever magical seal that had been closing the room off was no longer working.

The dust settled quickly, revealing the gigantic figure of the grey alien that Tempest, The Chimera King, had killed in front them.

Chapter 47

On a planet that's name had long since been lost to history in the outer fringes of the Milky Way, the environment was so harsh that life struggled to form. As with most life bearing planets, the first few single-called organisms failed to develop. Unlike most planets, this trend continued trillions of times over.

There were hundreds of reasons this happened. The air of the planet was poisonous almost all carbon-based life forms. The surface temperature of the planet had harsh extremes in temperature that fluctuated daily. The planet also had frequent gas storms which caused it to have rains of solid diamonds.

Despite the impossibility, a species of bacteria managed to develop further. A second species formed after that. Millions of generations later, the first aquatic animal species developed. This first species was a small fish. It was quickly made extinct by the second species, a jellyfish like species.

It was at this point in the planet's pre-history that the universe's first magical adaptation was discovered. Every species that the jellyfish-like species made extinct, had it's own abilities added to the jellyfish-like species. From the fish, they gained a sense of sight.

Eventually the jellyfish-like species killed or ate most species in the planet's ocean. This forced the planet's first amphibians to develop. Unfortunately, the jellyfish-like species, which now had developed to resemble sharks with jellyfish tentacles on their backs, managed to eradicate a small amphibious species. This caused the species to develop the ability to walk on land. The next species to be eradicated was a species of plant, which granted photosynthesis to the once jellyfish-like species.

Billions of years and millions of eradicated species later, the once-jellyfish like species was competing with the planet's other dominant bipeds. This was the first war of the nameless planet. It took multiple generations but eventually, the other bipeds were eliminated. Their gifts became part of the dominant species, including intentionally using magic.

By now the once jellyfish like species was comprised of gigantic gray humanoids with red eyes and hundreds of holes in their skin for retractable spikes and tendrils. They didn't eat. They didn't sleep. They had no worries for safety on their planet.

Thousands of years passed and they developed a society independent of the Kingdom of the Flock, which they were completely unaware of. Unlike Earthlings, their society wasn't plagued by wars or even internal violence. They had theater. They had poetry. They had advanced systems of healthcare that blended science and magic.

Soon, the species set out to spread their society. They traveled to other planets and attempted to peacefully convince them to leave the Kingdom. It was always to no avail. Each time being told how the humans of Earth offered the best protection. The species resolved itself to travel to Earth, the human Homeworld.

This journey is when one of the smallest of the species, a male named Vikask'rr was sent on his first off world mission. Vikask'rr was a kind man. He had been in a relationship for a few years but had no children. He was a soldier, but he had a passion for toys and games. Each break from duty, he would visit orphanages and play games with his homemade marbles.

Vikask'rr had killed animals but never another intelligent species. When the announcement was made that their trip to Earth had changed from a peaceful introduction to a full-scale invasion, Vikask'rr feared what would happen. There were billions more Earthlings than there were of his species, the "Gray Aliens" as the Earthlings referred to them.

The Gray Aliens elected to send every man, woman, and child to Earth to assist with the invasion. Vikask'rr wasn't sure what had happened to drive these rash decisions. The first few battles were successful. Vikask'rr breathed a sigh of relief with each destroyed city or surrendered town.

Then one day it all ended in a flash. A group called The Gaggle of The Knights of the Flock were distributed and with a single flash of light all of the

Gray Aliens Vikask'rr could see were dying before him. The Gaggle killed rest of the Gray Aliens by hand in what was a truly one-sided battle.

Vikask'rr fell with his species. His memories faded away. His love. His passions. Everything that made him an individual was gone. He laid on the ground hoping for his death. With his dying strength he wept uncontrollably. He did not want to die. He felt that he had so much left to live for. Strangely enough, the thought crossed his mind that he would never be able to play with his marbles again.

"You don't need to die you know." The voice came from his head but it was not his voice. It wasn't even speaking his language. It spoke the Earthling language.

"I don't?" Vikask'rr asked in his native tongue.

"No." the voice said, "You can serve me. You will never die again."

"Will I be able to avenge my people?"

"I'll help you."

In the last decision he ever made, Vikask'rr agreed to serve The Chimera King. And then Vikask'rr, the Gray Aliens, and their entire way of life was lost forever.

In Vikask'rr's place was Silverback, the last Gray Alien, the first Beast Knight. He dutifully did everything The Chimera King asked. In the event that he died in a mission, The Chimera King would revive him.

With each revival, Silverback lost a bit more of Vikask'rr. He lost his memories of his family. He lost his memories of his childhood. He lost everything but combat training and his love of small, round objects that he could play with. The only thing he cared about was keeping The Chimera King, his king, on the path to achieving their goals.

Decades passed until Silverback found himself in his current predicament.

Silverback wasted no time. He grabbed Crow, The Chimera King's son, his master's son, by the skull. He pressed his thumb onto the small half-elf's eye. If Crow was a lesser target, he would have collected that very eyeball to play with later. It was an honor that he was the one sent to capture Crow.

The other man in the room, lunged at Silverback. Silverback stopped the attack by grabbing the man by the throat. He began squeezing as the man tried to struggle free.

"Don't kill him." The Chimera King's voice in Silverback's head said, "bring them both to me."

Crow managed to push himself free from Silverback's grip. A magical door opened that Silverback could only assume was summoned by Crow. A pink woman, a small demon in a pinstripe suit, and a pink Golem erupted from the door.

The Golem kicked Silverback in the chest, forcing him to release the other man.

"Crow, Raven, are you alright?" The woman said as she helped Crow to his feet.

Silverback knew he couldn't win this situation if they completely regrouped. Without realizing that he was thinking autonomously, he grabbed both men by the skull and shouted, "I. Have. Them."

The world around him faded into dust. Within a second, Silverback, Raven and Crow were standing on a pile of dead mice.

They were in a castle, but not like the gilded castle of The Drakon King. This castle was decorated with jade and onyx. In front of the walls were granite statues of various beasts, both Earthling and Alien. There were no paintings. Directly before Silverback was an empty, black throne. This was the castle on Planet Doom.

"I brought you here with no real drain on my magic. The Chimera King will be pleased." Lioness said as she reached down and picked up one of the dead mice. She waved her hand and a pair of magical bindings appeared on Crow and Raven.

Silverback picked up both of his prisoners. They were lighter than he'd thought they would be. He imagined how easily their bones could be broken. If he squeezed tight enough, he was certain he could shatter their skulls like a lightbulb. He wouldn't dare though. He would never risk injuring perfectly good eyeballs.

Each step Silverback took while carrying the prisoners was answered with the scurry of smaller creatures that were crawling over the Beast Knight's castle. Silverback contemplated eating them but never had enough time to do so.

"I am pleased with you Silverback." The Chimera King said in his mind as Silverback entered the room and dropped the prisoners on the floor. Silverback smiled. He was elated. The Chimera King was pleased with him. He was going to remove the eyeballs of one of the prisoners as a celebration.

186

"Dismissed Silverback" The Chimera King said to him.

Silverback contorted his face to try to conceal his joy. He turned and marched out of the room. Once out of view he stopped to pick up a small, eight-legged mammal and ate it whole.

Chapter 48

"A lot of elves detest humans. A dog is to a human as a human is to an elf. Humans are less evolved. Humans live a fraction of the time an elf lives. I am not of that ilk. Dozens, maybe hundreds of my children follow this mindset. My parents certainly did. My aunts did. My uncles did. But I love humans."

The Chimera King was talking from his throne as Raven and Crow remained bound on the floor.

"My first love was a human. But the times were cruel and elves had her killed. We had a daughter. Elves had my daughter killed. They forced me to adapt to Elven life. I married an elf. We had dozens of children. But she knew what it was. I became an open secret. I bred with other elves. I bred with orcs. I bred with humans. The entire time, trying to exact a small amount of embarrassment on the elves that cost me my happiness for their enjoyment. And then, I killed my wife and all my concubines. Except your mother, the ship failure did that for me."

The Chimera King stood up from his throne. A servant bearing a red seal walked up to him holding a tankard of a deep red liquid. He took a long drink from it. The liquid dropped down the sides of his mouth. Another servant came and dried his face off.

"When I was about two, maybe three hundred, I decided that I would join The Flock. Back then, joining the flock meant that you chose to erase all of your memories, you chose to forego all previous relationships, your name was even erased and replaced magically. My father was the Arch Mage under the Wyvern King. Just as I was prepared to leave his and my family's misery behind, he altered the spell that creates the Knighting Ritual. So, I became stuck with every ounce of pain that I tried to escape. That's why Raven. That's why you have clear vivid memories of your father's death. That's why Crow. That's why you can feel the sadness of losing your mother every day. That's why I feel the sadness of losing my daughter. The only thing we've lost is our names now."

The Chimera King sat back down. The expression on his face was one of sincere sadness. The frown on his lips curled into a smile.

"That is why I reveled in the fact that he was sentenced to death for his rebellion. Why I laughed when the elves tried to revolt against The Flock and were subsequently slaughtered. Yes, many elves may believe they are superior to humans. But at least now there's less of them." The Chimera King stood up again and walked down to Crow and Raven. He sat between them on the floor. The two exhausted knights could do nothing in response.

"And then the Wyvern King died a thousand years ago so that an entire generation could learn how kings are chosen. At first, we expected it to be one of his children, but the Gold Seal never appeared under any of their eyes. They checked every single child in the kingdom. They finally found a boy in an orphanage on one of Earth's colonies on the moons of Jupiter. You know him as The Drakon King."

The Chimera King gently placed his hands on the backs of his captured audience.

"You can imagine my surprise when a few years ago, I woke up with a Gold Seal of my own. I am a King. I am destined to rule. I am destined to bring the change I want to see to universe. But most importantly, I can punish the society that made me the way I am. I will eradicate the races of man and the citizens of the stars and make them all Beast Knights. They'll all be powerful. They'll all superior. Because when everyone's superior, nobody is."

He turned his gaze downward.

"And so, I'm finally at you. Crow and Raven. My son and my pupil. The Half Elf with the rare and powerful summoning magic. The human with Anti-Magic. I want you to be my first generals. The Flock has the wind; I want you to be the planet."

Suddenly a crash of doors into the hall sounded like a shotgun. While Crow and Raven couldn't see Silverback enter the room, they could feel the tremor of every step he made.

"I'm.... Sorry... Chimera King..." Silverback choked out. "I... Should... Be... A General."

"Silverback. Is this a free thought." The Chimera King said, "I didn't know you were capable of such a thing."

"I... Will... Kill... Everything... For The Chimera King."

"Tell me more Silverback."

"I... Can... Talk..." Silverback said, "I... Can... Fight..."

"How would you deal with a mutiny?" The Chimera King asked.

"I would kill... every one of them..." Silverback said with much more ease, "Then... Make... New... Beast Knights."

"It would be fantastic for the other Beast Knights to see one of their own made into a general. I'll tell you what Silverback. You can have a trial by combat with these two gentlemen. If you impress me, you can be a general. What say you Crow and Raven?"

Crow and Raven's mouths were unbound.

"We will never join the Beast Knights, father." Crow replied.

"Very well then." The Chimera King said, "Silverback will just kill you both then."

Chapter 49

Puffin was in a room with Penguin, Kiva, and Mirai. Mirai had only minutes before gotten Kiva released from holding using diplomatic immunity. The four of them were a mess. Puffin was admittedly his normal sweaty self, but Penguin, Kiva, and Mirai were not the image of happiness or stability.

Kiva in particular looked different. She wasn't wearing her civilian clothes and was instead wearing tactical gear of Aesop's private army. The gear was far less bulky than what the Knights of the Flock wore. It was a deep blue color consisting of pants, a tight-fitting shirt, and a protective vest. Tied to left hip was a black bag that Puffin had seen members of the Flock use to keep magical tools in. On her right hip was small laser gun, Puffin would be amazed if the weapon could pull off a single round.

In contrast Puffin and Penguin were wearing their commander's armor set. It was bulky, silver, and they had both modified it to suit their needs. Puffin had adorned his armor with runes of protection both inside and out. He had shown Penguin how to do the same; while she did draw runes of protection, on her wrists and thighs were runes of strength and accuracy.

Mirai was not dressed for combat. She was clearly dressed for diplomacy. Though her wild hair and messy makeup betrayed her purpose for being in the room. She had visibly paused for what Penguin explained were visions of the future.

The door to the room opened for the Knight Captains and their lieutenants, Royal Guard, and The Drakon King. All of whom were wearing their commander's armor.

"Penguin, I'm so glad you're allowed at these things." Swan said before the meeting officially started.

Swan had dyed her hair an electric pink color. As she was a poet, Puffin was convinced that she had divined some explanation for the radical change. While it made her look less intimidating, it wasn't masking who she was at all. Swan was the only mage that possessed the power of Page Magic in the Flock. Anything she wrote on her paper would come to pass as long as she could clearly imagine it. She once stood before an army of NRLs alone and wrote a poem about the NRLs turning to autocanibalism. Before help could arrive, the NRLs had eaten each other and themselves.

Swan brought rain to deserts, cured life threatening injuries, and altered reality in ways that few could have comprehended. Puffin could comprehend it. Swan was practically a goddess, the only thing stopping her was her dedication to artistry. Often times, she refused to reuse spells or act purely out of malice. When reports surfaced of her Squad mates abusing their power, Swan wrote the offending members into trees.

Of all the Knights of the Flock, Swan was the only one that actually terrified Puffin. As a fellow lieutenant, they had worked together for years. But they were nowhere near the same. Swan was genuinely friendly and by all accounts a fair leader, but her magical abilities were beyond any mage except for The Drakon King. Her standing as the top of the Kill Count was proof enough.

"No small talk." Goose grumbled.

"Yes sir." Swan replied before turning toward Penguin and whispering, "we'll catch up later."

Where Swan was responsible with her power, Goose was intimidatingly irresponsible. He had no known magical ability, but he did have something special, durability. Goose had been shot, stabbed, and attacked magically and seemed to get away unscathed. Goose had never so much as missed a meeting. He expected the same of every member of the Gaggle. There were reports that punishments for breaking Goose's policy were extreme in the slightest of cases. Puffin was glad he'd never been assigned to that squad.

"Time is paused for this room." The Drakon King started, "I recently paused time to walk across the galaxy. I'd do it again, but I have reason to believe The Chimera King can neutralize or otherwise detect Time Magic."

"What makes you think that?"

"He has no future." Mirai interjected. "I've been trying to force myself to have visions. Nothing about him ever comes. Usually that means someone is dead but he's clearly still alive."

"I thought that you couldn't control your visions?" Puffin asked.

"The Drakon King has been helping me. My visions are an expression of Time Magic."

"And you're doing quite well Your Regency," The Drakon King said, "I gathered you all here to strategize about the war."

"Wait what about Crow and Raven?" Kiva said.

"Excuse me?" Blue Jay said, "I don't believe you are a Knight or a Royal. You should know your place."

"Or I could talk because I only take orders from Mirai"

"Your Regency," Blue Jay said, "Control your servants."

"I'm not an elf. We don't believe in servants or slaves. She's my sworn protector."

"Calm down." The Drakon King ordered, "We cannot afford to send an invasive force to The Chimera King for two Knights."

"So, we're leaving them to die?" Penguin said angrily.

"You dare question The Drakon King?" Goose replied.

"Goose sir," Swan said calmly, "She is not questioning the The Drakon King so much as she is protecting her friend."

"Thank you, Swan." Penguin said.

"The Flock won't waste any ships." Mirai said. "Aesop will be sending a small ship with the express purpose of rescuing Crow and Raven."

"Aesop has no navy or pilots." Blue Jay said, "You're barely a state in The Drakon Kingdom. I will not be sending any of my ships or pilots to this mission."

"I will get a ship and pilot." Mirai said, "I just need a few soldiers."

"I volunteer" Penguin said.

Puffin could feel the guilt creeping into him like a stomach ache. "I volunteer."

"If you're both gone, who will handle the day-to-day operations of The Charm?"

"I can share Swan with you. Then she can whip your squad into shape."

"It's settled then." The Drakon King said.

Chapter 50

Puffin was on a ship with Penguin, Charly, Mirai, and Kiva. The ship was a speeder bearing no markings or signals of the Flock. Goose had explained to Penguin before they left that this was a covert operation and would there for not be acknowledged by The Flock. They were to go to the Beast Knight's Planet, grab Raven and Crow and return to Homeworld as fast as possible.

"It's a good thing Charly got her pilot's license." Penguin said.

Puffin clenched his seat and said, "yeah this is great," through gritted teeth.

"Your Regency, are you sure you couldn't have a Flock pilot bring us to our destination?"

Mirai frowned, "I'll be honest when you're honest."

"What do you mean?"

"You're a Beast Knight." Mirai said, "You're going to betray the Flock and there's nothing you can do about it."

Puffin stopped everything he was doing. He had been outed as the enemy. He questioned whether or not he was in trouble.

"Relax. We know you're not in charge of your affliction." Mirai said calmly.

"But we also know if you're leading us into a trap," Kiva said, "I'll personally summon a Golem to smash you into paste."

"So why did you trust me for this?" Puffin asked.

"To get to Suge, you need a Red Seal." Penguin said plainly, "It has nothing to do with trust at least on their end. That area of space is crawling with Beast Knights."

"Hey, I have a question," Mirai said, "If you're a Beast Knight, why isn't your name Chimpanzee or something?"

"I honestly don't know. The Beast Knights don't talk much. They all communicate psionically with each other. Though most of them weren't great speakers before they were conscripted."

"So can you do whatever you want?"

"No." Puffin said, "I can't commit suicide. I can't attack any of the Beasts. I can't even think about hurting The Chimera King. Not that I could. There's powerful and then there's the Kings."

They flew in silence for a few minutes before Charly stood up from the controls, grabbed a set of restraints, and fastened them to Puffin's arms and legs.

"I'm not a Knight" Charly said as she pulled the restraints as tight as she could, "I can't do Magic. I don't have any desire to fight anyone. In all honesty, I'm only here because no one else can fly a Speeder that is available. I know you're saying you mean well. But I don't know you and I don't trust you."

Puffin frowned. Charly was right not to trust him. Even though he was being as honest as he could be, The Chimera King could have been manipulating his thoughts and actions."

"I don't blame you." Puffin said.

"You don't get it." Charly said, "I watch my girlfriend and most of my friends go into danger every single day. You're literally the danger. I'm only flying you because for some reason Penguin still trusts you. But make no mistake, I will leave you there."

They flew in silence for a few more minutes.

"Kiva," Mirai said to break the silence.

"I want you to reach out to Owl and Condor. If we aren't back within a certain timeframe. I want them to pick us up"

"That's not how it works." Penguin said, "they're in different units"

"They're low-level grunts with a ton of time off accumulated because you're all workaholics. I had them schedule today off weeks ago."

The ship's engine died.

"We're in Beast Space." Puffin said. He felt emotionally numb as if he couldn't feel anything.

A Destroyer appeared from thin air.

"Since when do Destroyers have cloaking tech?" Penguin asked.

"Since today apparently." Charly replied.

An image appeared on the comm screen. It was a young woman with frizzy hair and a red seal under her left eye. Her gaze was intimidating even though Puffin knew she was staring at a camera. Behind her was a large boy and a smaller girl. A second boy with blue skin was sitting behind them.

"I am Lioness, commander of this ship." The young woman said, "you are clearly in Beast space. Identify yourself."

"I am Puffin. Beast Knight stationed on Earth. I have to see our Master."

"The Chimera King is busy. You should know that."

"I know but things that I'm doing are pertinent right now."

"What is per..tin..ent?" Lioness asked. For a brief moment it was clear that she was struggling to learn and have free thoughts like most of the other Beast Knights.

"It means important."

"How many of us can use that word?"

Puffin paused. He suddenly was able to see who knew what among the Beast Knights. Suddenly he was terrified. Every Beast Knight could see what he knew if they questioned it.

"Me and you now." Puffin answered.

"When will The Drakon King invade Suge?"

"I do not know."

Lioness paused then said, "None of us know."

"How long have you been at command?"

"Today." Lioness said, "The Chimera King realized how intelligent I am and used me."

"May we enter?"

"Yes." Lioness said then disabled the monitor.

Puffin turned toward Charly and said, "I know the coordinates of The Chimera King."

Chapter 51

"I'll kill you!" Silverback shouted as he squeezed Crow's throat and slammed him down to the ground. They were in what was a sports arena on Suge. The sound Crow made as his body bounced off the floor was one of pure agony. They had been fighting for a few minutes and it was clearly one sided.

Raven rushed in and tried to attack from behind. Silverback extended the spikes on his back and nearly impaled Raven. This was easy.

"Use your magic." Raven said to Crow.

"I'm trying." Crow shouted back.

Crow tackled and drove his shoulder into Silverback's ankle. Silverback toppled and crashed into the ground. The two Knights of the Flock piled on top of the Beast Knight. He extended the spikes in his chest. This time he pierced the skin of Raven.

"Do you two know the history of Grey Aliens?" The Chimera King shouted down to Crow and Raven as Silverback punched Raven in the jaw.

"There were two attempted invasions of Earth. One was Martians. The other was Grey Aliens. It took a nuclear warhead to stop the Grey Aliens and even then several still lived. Nobody knows where they came from, why they invaded Earth, what their society was like. But they were the most effective soldiers in history. I had to have one for my army. So, I scoured the universe for an intact corpse and made him into Silverback."

Raven round kicked Silverback in the stomach. Silverback didn't allow himself to flinch. He knew that this stage of the battle was all mental. If he could break his opponent's will, their bodies would wither. He caught a follow up kick from Raven and threw Raven across the field.

A magical door opened in the middle of the field and what looked like five thousand hands cane flying out. Some of them attacking Silverback. Some of the hands were shielding the two knights. Silverback extended his spikes and skewered dozens of hands. They dropped to ground. Though they were immediately replaced with more hands.

Try as he might, Silverback knew that the wave of hands would need to be stopped from the source. He would need to close the magical door.

He marched toward the door despite the grabbing at his ankles, weighing him down. A disembodied head floated from the door and stared Silverback in the eye as the hands grasped and contorted around it until they formed a giant, humanoid shape. It was a golem made of hands.

"Since when can you do that?" Raven yelled.

"Since right now." Crow said.

A second golem, this one made of stone with two heads emerged from the door.

Silverback retreated from the door and changed his focus. He ran to Raven and punched the knight of the Flock in the jaw. He extended a spike toward Raven's throat. At that exact moment he was felled by a stone fist to back of the head.

Silverback looked up from the ground to see the gigantic two headed golem standing above him. It rained down a flurry of heavy punches that allowed Raven to scramble away. As Silverback finally regained his bearings and began to defend himself he was attacked by the Hand Golem.

The Hand Golem broke itself apart and reformed around Silverback. Once Silverback was trapped, the hands surrounding him scratched, clawed, and punched the Beast Knight an immeasurable number of times.

Silverback would not break. Letting out a mighty roar, he extended every spike on his body. He pierced as many of the hands as he needed. Soon enough he was standing in a pile of hands with a disembodied head laying in front of him. Silverback reached down at the head and pulled out its eyeballs with his gigantic grey fingers. The eyes instantly regenerated.

He smiled. The eyes in his hand were blue. The regenerated eyes were purple. He placed the blue eyes in his bag then looked back at the purple eyes. He plucked the purple eyes too. They regenerated brown and were plucked. They

198

were red and were plucked. This went on long enough that Silverback almost forgot that he was in a battle.

He cast a quick gaze at Crow and Raven. They were talking but weren't moving. The two headed golem had begun fighting itself. He wasn't afraid. Nothing had seriously hurt him. All Silverback wanted to do was sit down and collect the magical eyeballs.

Chapter 52

"Numcustos Bestia," Crow said quietly, "Ladon Chronosimi."

Two very small magical doors opened. Numcustos and Simi snuck out as quietly as they possibly could. Not that it mattered, Silverback was completely distracted. Crow was fortunate that the hands and the head regenerated. Though their magical energy was spent for the most part so he couldn't reform the Hand Golem or have them attack.

"What do we know about Grey Aliens?"

"That they have that species name because Earthlings have no sense of culture. Not that anyone knows anything about them."

"They don't like cold temperatures." Simi said. "I have a magical sword that freezes on contact in my realm that could be useful."

"Go get that." Raven said.

Simi didn't move, "You're not Crow or Kiva."

"Simi, go get the sword."

Simi disappeared into a magical door then reappeared immediately holding a long sword in his mouth. He dropped it at Raven's feet.

"Now what do we have that can create cold temperatures?" Crow asked.

"Timmy!" Crow and Numcustos said at the same time.

Numcustos opened a door and disappeared into it. A few seconds later a massive door opened in the middle of the field. Crow could feel the air instantly chill. A mist started to flow from the door. That's when the creature that Numcustos retrieved emerged.

It was definitely still an Ice Nought, but it was possibly the largest living creature that Crow had ever seen. It was a cool blue color, covered in ice and snow. On its back we're two cones of ice with a matching cone protruding from its chest. Each labored breath it took caused mist to flow from its mouth. Crow instantly regretted not paying more attention to Numcustos's stories about Timmy.

Timmy slightly lifted its arm up and a row of icicles erupted from the ground. They stopped in front of The Chimera King who had nullified it with some sort of barrier.

"Timmy!" Crow shouted. "I order you to attack the Grey Alien known as Silverback."

Timmy created more icicles which Silverback dodged. Timmy swatted at Silverback which caused the Grey Alien to go flying into the wall of the arena.

Silverback picked himself up and retreated backward only to run into an attack from Raven whom was now armed with the ice blade. While it didn't cut through Silverback's skin, ice spikes could be seen forming around the Beast Knight's chest.

Silverback howled in pain and jumped up in the air, over Raven.

Timmy encased Silverback in a block of ice from the neck down. Another howl erupted from Silverback as he hit the ground hard enough to leave a deep crater.

For the first time since he was imprisoned, Crow felt like he could get away from this entire situation alive. He smiled.

The smiled faded immediately as Silverback broke free of the ice and resumed his onslaught. He delivered a swift blow to Timmy that despite being blocked sent cracks up and down the Ice Nought's arms.

"Crow! Open a door beneath Timmy now." Numcustos shouted.

Timmy fell into the gate. To Crow's absolute surprise, the Gehenna Beast leapt out and pounced on Silverback.

"I did not do that." Numcustos Bestia said.

Silverback threw the Gehenna Beast off of him and turned his attention to Crow. As he charged forward, Silverback was met with Raven who cut his arm off with a smooth slash that Crow could only imagine took years to perfect. The wound immediately froze over.

Silverback picked his arm off the ground and stared at it in shock. He howled and threw the arm at Raven whom sliced it in half in midair.

Simi flew over and latched himself onto Silverback from behind. "I can age him." Simi said excitedly.

Crow tried to call Simi back but the sound was lost in the moment.

Simi was immediately thrown off Silverback but not before several of the spikes on his back withered and fell off. Silverback didn't howl. He instead charged forward with a spike extended from his wrist.

Silverback's spike broke through Raven's chest and went clear through his back.

Raven's sword followed a similar path.

Both warriors fell.

Chapter 53

Raven would be pronounced officially dead at 7:23 pm Galactic Standard Time. His cause of death would labeled, "in the line of duty." His body would be brought back to Earth. His mother would be presented a bouquet of flowers. Everyone he knew would cry, including Crow. He wouldn't buried. Burials were outlawed after the first NRL outbreak in the mid 2500's. Instead, he would be cremated and a hologram of him in his armor would be made available at any Hall of the Dead in the Kingdom for people to view. Because he was a Knight, there would be a service for him led by his squad captain. But his squad captain was now The Chimera King, so his service would be led by The Drakon King.

The Drakon King would give a speech about the tragedy of loss and promise to bring Silverback to justice. He would scratch his beard. He would cry. He would appear human instead of the god that his subjects perceived him to be. He would note how Crow fought to bring Raven back to Earth.

Crow would have been seated next to Kiva at the service. They would hold hands. Crow would have cried as much as he would hate to admit it. Crow would be wearing tape around his rips and a neck brace. He would go home to his strange family of his beloved, his dragon, and his Demidemon. They would try to cheer him up but nothing would work except for time.

Owl would pretend nothing was wrong. She was the strongest willed of all his friends. Though it would be a lie. After a couple weeks, Penguin and Owl would be sitting at Owl's house. They would go through pictures of Raven and cry their eyes out.

Condor would dedicate his first ship as "The Raven," of course it would be a battle ship designed to lead a charge into combat.

Mirai would at first frantically try to find a future where Raven wasn't dead. She would call friends to ask if they heard rumors. She would want Raven to be alive and she always got what she wanted until then.

After a year passed, all of Raven's friends would get together for a game night. Kiva would have an engagement ring on her finger as was Earth tradition and Crow would wear a crown on his head as was tradition on Aesop. The group would make fun of the crown which would upset Crow. They'd all laugh together like the old days. It was comforting to know things would continue after he was dead.

But Raven wasn't dead.

He wasn't ready to die. He could feel the cold start to envelope him from the inside. He panicked internally. Unable to move except for a tremble and stream of tears.

He felt Crow struggling to keep him alive with an emergency healing spell. It wasn't working.

"You're dying you know." A voice said in Raven's head, it was the all too familiar voice of The Chimera King. "My offer still stands. Silverback has died many times. I've always brought him back. I always bring back my Knights. You are all valuable to me. You don't need to die. All you need to do is accept my offer. Become a Beast Knight. You can even keep your chosen name. Just submit your will. You'll never need to fear death or failure again."

Another healing spell failed. Crow tried to cover the wound. Though Raven could feel it was only prolonging the inevitable.

"Join me, Raven. You don't need to die."

Crow started talking.

"Raven. I'm sorry I was so terrible to you." Crow said. "You're not useless. You're not stupid. If anything, I'm useless. I summoned things to fight for me, you fought yourself."

Raven couldn't answer.

Crow continued, "Raven, just hold on. We can make it. We can get out of here."

Crow opened a magical door.

"Crow," Numcustos Bestia said, "there's no way Raven could survive a trip through Gehenna in that condition."

204

"You're running out of time." The Chimera King said in Raven's mind.

"I..." Raven choked out.

"Save your strength." Crow said.

"I..." Raven said.

"What is it?" Crow said softly. Raven could feel that these were his last words.

"I accept your offer."

The Chimera King's voice in Raven's head began to ring louder.

"Asleep the weak. Arise the Beast." The Chimera King said in Raven's mind.

He could feel the magic flow through him. His wounds closed. His muscles spazzed and twitched. The warmth of life was slowly returning to his body as he felt an indescribable pain as if every cell in his body had just been punctured.

Just as quickly as the pain started, it subsided. He sat up and stared at Crow.

"Did my healing spell work?"

"No."

Crow took a step back.

A second searing pain burned its way from Raven's left eye, down to his jawline. The Red Seal had formed. He was now a Beast Knight.

"Kill him." The Chimera King said in Raven's mind.

Raven sprang up. Before his feet settled on the ground, the Gehenna Beast pounced on him and sank its teeth around his throat. Without thinking Raven used Wavelength to banish all of Crow's summoned minions and weapons back through magical doors. Leaving only the two of them and Silverback's corpse on the floor.

"We both knew this was our destiny," Raven said.

He was surprised. For as much as he had tried to befriend Crow, it was surprisingly easy to want to kill him. This was being a Beast Knight. It only occurred to him that he had perfect control over his Anti-Magic.

Crow kicked Raven in the stomach then shot a takedown. Raven sprawled to defend and dropped all of his weight on the back of Crow's neck. Crow pushed through but Raven was able to transition the takedown attempt into a choke. Crow defended and retreated.

A magical door opened. Raven shut the door.

A single hand flew toward Raven's face. Raven caught it then looked Crow in the eye as he broke its middle finger.

"You shouldn't be mad. I learned that finger break from watching you."

Crow ran to the entrance tunnel and managed to open a door for a Minotaur to come out swinging a giant cleaver. Raven reacted by instinctively using Wavelength to send the Minotaur back to Gehenna.

They were at a stalemate. Raven couldn't beat Crow in hand to hand combat and Crow couldn't use magic to gain the upper hand. If Raven managed to get his hands on any sort of weapon, he would have been able to end Crow and make The Chimera King pleased with his performance.

Chapter 54

Above the stadium there was a dog fight. Puffin realized that he no longer got air sick while evasive maneuvers occurred. It felt like he was in his twenties again.

"Charly. This ship has no weapons." Penguin said while clutching a rail.

"I'm well aware of that." Charly said.

"Well don't crash the ship." Penguin yelled.

"Do you want to drive?" Charly said in an annoyed tone.

"No." Penguin backed down.

"Thought so."

There were a few panicked moments of silence before the ship lurched forward throwing everyone that was on board from their balance. The monitors were displaying bright red notifications that they'd been hit.

"Hey Penguin." Mirai said, "I thought you should know the ship is going to crash in a minute or so."

"No, we're not." Charly yelled back.

The ship was hit again.

Puffin didn't need to look at the monitor to see that they were hurtling to the ground, Puffin almost laughed. He watched from his bound place as the rest of the travelers braced for impact.

The ship crashed directly into a stadium as if it were pulled down magnetically. Puffin could feel The Chimera King. There wasn't time to process. Penguin rushed past on her way out of the ship followed by Kiva whom disappeared into the distance.

Mirai was also moving frantically but stopped long enough for Puffin to see that she was bleeding from the side of her head. A small blue Golem that Kiva had apparently left behind was tending to her wounds. Once it finished, the Golem walked past Puffin and flashed him the middle finger on the way to addressing other people's injuries.

That was when Puffin heard the scream. He stood up and looked around to see Penguin sitting on the floor next to Charly. It was immediately apparent what had happened, Charly was injured more severely in the crash than the others.

"Golem. Compress the wound." Mirai ordered, "Charly it's going to be okay. I sent Kiva to rescue Crow and Raven and we're all going to be fine."

"You know that for sure?" Penguin asked, she had a tone of desperation in her voice.

"I know that Charly has a future." Mirai said.

Penguin's body language relaxed slightly. Puffin got close enough to see that Charly was bleeding profusely from her abdomen and had lost consciousness either from pain or blood loss.

"Puffin, I'm going to send the signal for Owl and Condor to come get us. You and Mirai stay here and try to get the bleeding to stop." Penguin ordered.

"Shouldn't you stay here and have me or Mirai request help?"

"As much as I love you both, you're still a Beast Knight and I don't know that I can trust you on communications, and I don't have the time to explain to Mirai how to work the system. I am doing this right and I am doing this now."

Puffin and Mirai lifted Charly out of the cockpit and brought her to a space where they could lay her down comfortably. The reluctant Beast Knight felt a tug in the back of his mind to kidnap the Regent of Aesop and bring her to The Chimera King. As he always did, he resisted The Chimera King's temptations.

It was at this moment that Puffin realized his exact location. The ship had crash landed in The Chimera King's personal stadium. He wouldn't be able to fight the temptation. The walls felt as if they were closing in around him as he began to violently hyperventilate. He fought the urge to vomit. He fought the urge to grab Mirai and take her. He fought the urge to kill Charly. He fought the urge to kill Penguin.

Puffin grabbed his own head with both hands and yelled out as loud as he could. He took a step toward The Chimera King but stopped.

"Puffin." Mirai said in a tone barely above a whisper.

"Raven turned on the Flock." Puffin said before saying what he was slowly realizing, "I can't fight it anymore."

"Puffin." Mirai said. She looked at him with an expression that conveyed sympathy, "I already know what's going to happen."

"What's going to happen?" Puffin said. He could feel his eyes welling with tears.

"You're going to turn on the Flock." Mirai said calmly and quietly.

"I would never." Puffin was now crying. Streams of tears had ruined whatever makeup he still had on.

"You don't have a choice." Mirai said, "I'm not going to stop you. You're his now. But I have one thing to ask."

"What?" Puffin asked.

"I want to order your last act as a Knight of the Flock, or your first act as a Beast Knight, I don't entirely know how these things work. I just order them." Mirai said as her eyes welled up with tears, "I want you to save Charly. I have seen several futures where she dies right here. But I've seen some where you save her. You can do it."

The medical Golem collapsed. Kiva was either incapacitated or had diverted her magical power elsewhere. Puffin tried to think of other options. He drew a blank. He didn't know any medical runes that would work on another person. Compressing the wound would only work for so long.

"You have a problem Puffin." The voice of The Chimera King was like gunfire in the back of Puffin's mind.

"Mirai," Puffin said as he began sobbing uncontrollably, "I'm so sorry. Tell Penguin I'm sorry. Tell them all I'm sorry."

"Will you finally join me?" The Chimera King said in a tone that couldn't hide his happiness.

"I will on one condition." Puffin thought as hard as he could, "You save Charly."

"Doing this will doom her to a fate that you have been trying to avoid." The Chimera King said. Puffin could imagine The Chimera King smiling widely at this entire situation.

"I understand, but there's no other way." Puffin said, this time out loud.

He didn't feel himself teleport. But he was suddenly in a large, poorly lit Destroyer. Beside him, bearing a glowing red seal under his left eye was Raven.

At his feet was the dying Charly. Surrounding them were hundreds of Beast Knights whom had begun working on the ship as soon as they gathered their bearings from teleportation. The crowd began to clear as the lights began to illuminate the ship. Monitors came to life showing everything that they had just left on Suge. It was clear that the only people left were the Flock. Puffin struggled to hold back tears.

"Raven, Puffin." The familiar voice of The Chimera King said to them. "Now that I have you both here. I saw no point in remaining on Suge, did you?"

"What about Charly?" Puffin said.

"Oh yes," The Chimera King said, "Asleep the weak, awaken the Beast."

Charly's eyes popped open as if she were jolted from a nap and not a near death experience.

"I am so sorry Charly." Puffin said.

"You don't get to call me that anymore," Charly said as her seal began to slowly form under her eye, "Nobody does. I'm Otter now."

The newly christened Otter stood up and cast Puffin the coldest glance that he had ever seen before walking off. Puffin decided it was best not to follow after her despite wanting nothing more than to beg for her forgiveness.

Their lives were over.

"So, are you still Raven?" Puffin said as he turned to his former subordinate.

"I am." Raven replied, "Are you still Puffin."

"No." Puffin said, "Puffin died a while ago. I guess, I've been pretending to be him. But you can call me Vole now."

The pair fell silent as they accepted their fate as Beast Knights. They were now the enemy. Not only that, but they had decided to become the enemy. Vole was certain he no longer had a home to return to. Vole and Raven stared at a monitor that showed the void of space. He wondered if Raven felt the void like he did.

Vole regretted every decision he had made since turning into a Beast Knight, except for saving Otter.

He stared at a monitor that was displaying Suge to see a ship land on the field with a small force of machines picking up Crow, and leading all the other members of the Flock to the ship. The machines were clearly Dwarven built which meant that Condor had managed to rescue everyone. Vole wondered what

210

would have happened if he'd waited a few more moments.

Chapter 55

Three weeks in the hospital felt like an eternity. Even with magical healing. Crow still required every minute of time. The entire time he was in bed, Kiva never left his side.

"Tell me again how you found me." Crow said.

"Pay attention this time." Kiva said, "You and Raven were passed out. Then Raven disappeared. Puffin, Charly, and Silverback disappeared too."

"Your face scrunched when you said Charly and Puffin."

"It felt wrong to call them those names."

"They're probably Beast Knights now." Crow said before pausing.

He thought about the occasions where Penguin had come to visit. Every account about her status was that she was devastated by the disappearance of her best friend and her lover. For the first time in his life, Crow felt sadness for another person.

"You know," Crow said to Kiva, "Raven was probably my best friend. I wonder if I had been kinder to him if he would have gone to join the Beasts."

"You can't question that." Kiva said, "Raven and Puffin decided what they did by themselves."

"So, what now?"

"Now you take your medicine and rest. The Drakon King wants to see you as soon as your well. Mirai had a vision that will affect the turn of this war."

Chapter 56

"You wanted to see us sir?" Crow asked nervously.

Nervous wasn't something he generally experienced, though something about being an intergalactic fugitive and witness to multiple Knight defections to an enemy force helmed by his own father seemed to bring the nervousness out of Crow.

Sitting beside Crow was Penguin whom had an eerie calm about her given the situation. Like Crow, she was unbound, not that a binding would matter for either of them. More notable was how exhausted she looked. Crow wondered if he looked the same. Her attention was turned toward the figure at the head of the table.

Surprisingly, The Drakon King was smiling. It was a stark contrast to somber nature of their meeting. Crow wondered if The Drakon King smiled while he executed people. This was a man that authorized a confirmed kill count as something to celebrate. This was a man that turned his Knight Commanders into some of the biggest celebrities in history.

Crow's mind wandered toward the fact that there was no data anywhere on The Drakon King's fighting style. No recorded altercations. No listed combat, except for one. He ended an entire invasion of Pluto in less than a minute. When locals tried to describe what happened, they couldn't. It was as if time stopped before the battle and fast forwarded to the end. Crow knew that was exactly what happened.

If this were an execution, Crow started to wonder, "Could Simi neutralize The Drakon King's Time Magic?"

"I did bring you here." The Drakon King said, his smile still present.

"May we ask why?" Penguin asked bluntly.

The Drakon King turned toward Crow, "How did you escape?"

"Numcustos Bestia... a Demidemon contracted to me helped me out." Crow said.

"And your tunneling method. Stacking doors and traveling between realms. How did you figure it out."

"It was a group effort borne from necessity."

"But how did you figure out the equation for the space and locations of the doors?" The Drakon King said, "I know it's in your training to give minimal answers. But consider every detail to be the minimum necessary here."

"I can't explain it. I just did it."

"And your capture spell. How do you know which runes and symbols to use to capture something like an Ice Nought?"

"I don't usually use runes. I learned early on that Runes should be reserved for the most powerful creatures. Timmy wasn't that powerful at the time."

"Entire teams of mages would argue that." The Drakon King said as he turned his attention to Penguin, "why is it, no matter what major event is happening you seem to be involved? No matter who we put you with they listen to you? I've never seen a knight with a stronger network in less than five years."

"It's because I get results your majesty."

"My advisors cannot be trusted. Truth be told, nobody knows who to trust anymore." The Drakon King lamented. "The Chimera King himself was my most trusted advisor. Nobody should trust anybody. But I have this theory. Set aside his personal vendettas and what The Chimera King truly wishes for is to control magic."

"So why hasn't he killed you yet?" Penguin asked.

"Because a King can't kill another King." Crow answered, "If he stabbed you, you'd rewind time. And if you stabbed him, his death magic would just revive him."

"It's simpler than that," The Drakon King said, "my golden seal won't allow me to kill anyone with a golden seal. I've tried."

"So, are you recruiting us to kill my father?" Crow asked.

"In a roundabout way, I am." The Drakon King said, "I want you two to be Knight Commanders."

Crow frowned, "I'm not exactly looking for a leadership position."

"Oh" The Drakon King said curiously. "Think about it."

Chapter 57

❝They called me The Drakon King because I was the most powerful mage to have ever been in the Flock. I should not have been chosen as king. I was born a commoner. I was born as a mixed-race child in a time where my existence was illegal. I was sickly and I was poor. When I found the Gold seal under my eye, I disguised it. I hoped that it would go away. I prayed that Tempest would wake up with it. Slowly, I accepted that I was King. That I am King.❞

The Drakon King was speaking to the Knight Commanders, their lieutenants, the Royal Guard and Crow. It had been several weeks since their battle on Planet Suge. It was now common knowledge that Raven and Puffin were Beast Knights and thus, the enemy. Though only the people in the room knew that Puffin had been a Beast Knight for months before that.

"Not long ago, my prayers were answered and Tempest received a Gold Seal. He can even make his own Knights. But this was not at all what I envisioned. I'll admit. My strategy of not being very offensive with the Beast Knights was somewhere in the hope that The Chimera King and I could come to a peaceful agreement. I see now that that that isn't the case."

A hushed buzz of energy went around the table.

"After careful consideration, we will be going on the offensive." The Drakon King said. "But I do not want this entire discussion to be about my failures. I do not want this entire thing to be about war. I want to take some time to highlight and reward some of our brave Knights."

The Drakon King clapped his hands and a group of Squires walked into the room holding boxes. Behind the Squires, Kiva, Condor, and Owl entered.

"Firstly, I want to award a Medal of Integrity to Owl and Condor. They flew into enemy territory to rescue captured Knights that I honestly should have sent a force to rescue. In doing so, they were able to confirm something I'd feared. The Chimera King uses Death Magic to teleport. He also likely uses it for his Knighting ritual."

The Chimera King opened two of the boxes, pulled out the green and gold medals and placed them around the necks of the Dwarven Wizard and the Medical Knight. There was a brief round of applause from everyone in the room.

"Next, I want to do some important promotions. As of today we will be increasing our ranks. This means our squads will need to increase. Easter and Tornado will be leading small squads of whom will be assigned later. In addition, Swan, Penguin, and Crow will now be Knight Commanders of our newest full units, The Ballet, The March, and The Murder."

Crow was surprised. He was now a Knight Commander. Certainly, there were Knights more deserving of the honor.

"This is not a time to consider seniority. This is a time to consider ability. Swan is the most capable Knight on the battlefield with the exception of Goose. Penguin has proven time and time again that she knows exactly what to do and executes perfectly in high pressure situations when I mentioned to the Squad Commanders that I would be doing this, they all agreed upon Swan and Penguin. Which brings me to Crow. Crow was my own personal choice. I have a feeling Crow will be capable of great things."

Before he made his way to Earth, Crow would have thought that it took too long for him to achieve the rank of Squad Captain. At this point in time, all he could think about was how unprepared he was to lead a group of Knights.

The door creaked open again. Crow could see Mirai poking her head in.

"Is it my turn yet?" The Regent of Aesop said.

"Yes Mirai," The Drakon King answered.

"Good." She said, "I also have an announcement. My bodyguard has outgrown me. She's proven herself to be one for adventure and is certainly a powerful mage in her own right."

Mirai walked up to Kiva and directed her to stand up. They looked into each other's eyes as Mirai said, "I am abstaining my position as Regent of Aesop to move to Earth at the request of The Drakon King. That means, Kiva, if you want, you can be a Knight now."

Kiva looked around the room last looking at Crow.

Kiva and Mirai even without the tie of being Regent and sworn protector, were inseparable. For Kiva to consider knighthood was not an easy decision. While it would be a far better use of her talents, Crow wasn't sure Kiva would do it. The stare between Crow and Kiva became noticeable.

"It's your decision." Crow said abruptly, "stop looking at me."

"This is what I want." Kiva said, "I already have a name picked out."

"What is it?" The Drakon King asked.

"Kestrel." Kiva answered excitedly, "Will I need to start as a Squire?"

"Technically." The Drakon King said, "But I'm sure the person in charge will let you take the Test of Might immediately."

The room applauded. Everyone congratulated everybody and for a brief second, Crow forgot that Raven and Puffin had betrayed the Flock and that they were now entrenched in a war

"I have one more thing." Mirai said quietly before yelling, "Hey I'm talking."

The crowd stopped.

"I had a vision Your Majesty." Mirai said, "There are more Kings emerging, each with their own followers. The war will engulf everyone."

"How many?" The Drakon King asked. The smile on his face faded.

"Five, including yourself and the Chimera, each with their own Gold Seal. Which means they each have their own claim to rule."

And with that, Crow was aware of what was before him. The Drakon King was for the freedom and safety of his people. The Chimera King, wished to enslave all his subjects. He wondered what ideology the other kings had.

A quiet cold washed over the room. Even The Drakon King seemed lost for words.

To be continued in
The Chimera King

The Bestiary of The Drakon King as Written by the Magnanimous Numcustos Bestia

This should be written in alphabetical order but as I'm sure you realize; the alphabetical order was created with no real rhyme or reason other than some idiots' preferences. I will instead be writing this in order of my preferences.

First let's go over what you'll see in Crow's Plane of Gehenna.

Numcustos Bestia: I'm starting with the best. I mean who else would I start with? Visually I'm your standard Demidemon (more on those later.) I'm 29 inches tall, I wear three piece suits, I have horns and a pointy tail. When I'm in Gehenna I can shape shift though it takes a lot out of me. I'm also way more handsome than your average Demidemon, if you know what you're looking for. I'm sure it'll come out later how I met Crow, but I've known him since he was a little boy. I can tell you that I was cursed to be a servant by the big guy. I don't know what I did to piss him off. He also cursed me with the inability to stop talking. Crow's done a lot of work to fix that last part.

Demidemons: Helping me run this realm are these guys. Regular Demidemons. They look like me with much worse fashion sense. They used to run rampant on Earth. So when they returned to Gehenna, the big guy was none too happy. Crow doesn't deal with them too often. I sign his name on the birthday cards.

The Summoned Skull: Crow can summon this annoying chatterbox. It is literally what the name implies, a disembodied skull that was beheaded and couldn't pass to the next life. He's useless. Though he knows hundreds of jokes. I named him Lafayette.

The Thousand Hands of the Needy: This is a spell that every summoner learns at some point or another. The hands are more like ghosts. They're floating hands. Anytime someone dies while committing theft, a part of their spirit remains as a hand. It's a punishment. But they are awesome! Crow uses the Hands in very inventive ways. He builds bridges, he makes giant fists, he does a lot. As a mage gets more powerful, their spells get more powerful. Crow's hands will probably be able to blot out the sun.

Golems: Golems are made of Rocks, Metal, even organic material. Anything can be brought to life with a heartstone. Crow has made hundreds of these guys. For some reason, his go to is an orange two headed thing called Mad Man. Crow's Golems are nowhere near as impressive as Kiva's. Truth be told, Crow started using Golems to work on his ability to control magic.

Dummies: These guys are basically Golems, made of cloth and stuffing. Crow beats these things up for his Jiu Jitsu practice. I use them for some of the other creatures play things. They have a small society. They even have a support group that meets on Tuesdays.

The Gehenna Beast: The Gehenna Beast is a four legged creature that takes the shape of Earth Creatures. Our Gehenna Beast met a house cat about eighty years ago. So now we have a nine hundred pound housecat that breathes fire. Do you even want to know what that litter box is like?

Fire Nought: Nought's are humans that used magical artifacts beyond their capability. Once you become a Nought, you're basically a snarling monster. Crow collects Noughts instead of killing them. Our Fire Nought is named Daryl. Daryl is an avid jazz listener. He's also a nine foot tall man made of fire.

Ice Nought: Noughts sometimes retain portions of themselves when they transform. Not enough to say they're the same person but enough that they're slightly depressing to be around. That's our Ice Nought, Timmy. He's a giant made of ice.

Now we should get to the real monsters. These are the creatures that Crow either doesn't have or can't have in his Plane of Gehenna.

Lich: A Lich is a lord of the dead. They're essentially a Nought but much more powerful and intelligent. Liches are terrifying. But honestly if you can get past the essence of fear they can put into you as floating, talking, skeletons that can use any magic that they want; they are only mostly terrifying.

NRL's: Every year some moron decides to try and bring back the dead. Every year it goes awry. Every year, Necromantic Reanimated Lifeforms go around like a plague of locusts. They're mindless, slow, shuffling. Like Raven after a big meal. They're only a threat because they spread like a virus. They smell terrible.

Minotaur: Half-man. Half-bull. All poker cheat. These guys are actually super intelligent until they get angry. The minotaurs that Crow employ have some of the most lucrative contracts in his plane of Gehenna.

Dragon: Ugh. Dragons annoy me. They're all in love with being dragons. They're pure of heart or something like that. Anyway, Dragons exclusively focus on one type of magic. When they use it, it always looks like a flame thrower. Dragons bond magically. They also fart themselves awake.

Star Angels: They're gigantic pink sting rays that float through space. They are fun to look at.

Human: You're reading this. You're a human. You're boring and greedy. You started life unable to walk. You learned to walk. You learned to talk. You take 20 years to reach sexual maturity. You spread like an infestation across the galaxy. It may be due to some magical adaptation but when you encounter a species outside of Earth, you influence their development. That's why there are so many bipedal species across the universe, a few can even breed with humans. Humans suck.

Elf: The Elves of Earth are the most natural mages to have ever existed. Though I'll be honest they're stuck up. They're also nowhere near as creative as humans. Nowhere near as vicious as Orcs. Elves have pointy ears and tend to be taller than most people. Though that seems to be due to magical adaptation not necessarily natural growth. They also live for thousands of years. The big guy once told me never to cross an elf, I'll have an enemy all my days.

Dwarf: Dwarves are fun. They are the smaller of the Earthling races. They generally can't do magic so they became the greatest scientist ever. Most times Dwarves go from planet terraforming them and moving on. They're little, they have beards.

Orc: The Orcs were once a species with traits of both Dwarves and Elves. But reached a united pact to make themselves stronger with one of the first curses ever. Now they can rip the doors off of space ships. I'd say it was successful. They're nowhere near as intelligent as Humans or Elves. But boy can they break stuff. They also worship violence. Nobody knows how old an Orc can get because they prefer to die in combat.

Orc-Man: The greediness of humans knows no bounds. They lost a war to Orcs and developed magic to make their own people into Orcs. Hence Orc-Men. They're a bit smaller than regular Orcs but also a tinge smarter. They still worship violence.

Orc-Elf: The elves did the same thing as humans except the Orc-Elves can sometimes be mages. What's scarier than a monster truck coming at you? A loaded tank with a trigger happy driver. That's what the elves created. Here's a funny note, Orc-Men and Orc-Elves all joined the Orcs. The plan failed. Ha ha. Humans suck.

Aesopians: So there used to be two races of Aesopians. The originals and what was basically their answer to Orcs. They warred for generations and destroyed the surface of the planet. Eventually the smaller of the two races made their own Orcs. Unlike the story above, the third species was much more intelligent and wiped out the other two. This is why I'm terrified of Kiva.

Icicle: They're the abominable snowman and his crazy cousins. Seriously. White fur six armed creatures that have managed to eradicate the need for magic in a frozen wasteland.

Garuda: Bird People. They are giant birds with human proportions. They have no sense of humor and communicate through machines attached to their throats.

Cinder Bird: A burnt out Phoenix. When a Phoenix explodes and dies, it becomes a Cinder Bird. Then it sheds its black feathers, grows colorful feathers and boom we have a Phoenix.

Phoenix: A giant bird with wings of fire. People keep Pygmy Phoenixes as pets but very few actually see the real deal. These guys are elusive. But they aren't my white whale.

Leviathan: This is my white whale. The biggest magical beast. There's tale of a Leviathan as big as a planet. They're giant serpents that can decimate Galaxies. They can eat armies. I just want one. I ask every year if Crow will go on an expedition with me to capture a leviathan. But no. It's always an argument about how Crow could summon it or where he would keep it. I say it doesn't matter. With a Leviathan as a bargaining chip I could be made into a full demon. Imagine me, Numcustos Bestia, full demon, riding into battle on a leviathan. It'd be beautiful.

Grey Aliens: They were conquerors in the past. That's literally all I know about them.

Martians: Martians are the stereotypical Green Aliens. They are mostly farmers.

Saturnians: They look mostly like Earthlings. Except their eyes tend to be funk colors. Raven has a picture of himself and some Saturnian woman as his cellphone background. Raven has not had a relationship since a relationship had him.

Demons: One day, if I do everything I'm supposed to. I'll be a full demon. Then I'll show ya.

Dramatis Personae

Knights of the Flock

Squires

"Fledglings though we may be, we shall protect the people"

Raven - A top tier Squire, a swordsman of common blood. Utilizes tools and training to overcome his own weaknesses. A human.

Crow - A top tier Squire, a Summoning Mage of Noble blood. Possesses multiple unique abilities. Can summon creatures from another dimension. Can summon and control Golems.

Penguin - A top tier Squire, a squad commander in training of common blood. A human. Uses magical runes to fortify her natural abilities.

Condor - A top tier Squire, the first known dwarven Mage. Possesses the unique ability to control machinery and technology.

Ostrich - A top tier Squire, a berserker of common blood. An Orc-Man.

Swallow - A top tier Squire, an Earth Mage of Noble blood. An Orc-Elf.

Cassowary - A top tier Squire, a berserker of common blood. An Orc.

Owl - A top tier Squire, a medical specialist. A human. Uses magic to fortify her natural abilities.

Loon - A top tier Squire with a history of acts of violence.

Turtledove - A top tier Squire, a mage with an air of superiority. A human.

Budgerigar - A mid-tier Squire.

The Charm
"Never stop moving"

Humming Bird- Knight Commander. A Swordswoman and Mage of Noble Blood. An elf.

Toucan - A top tier Knight. A swordsman of Noble blood. A human.

Puffin - A mid-tier Knight. Knight in Charge of all Squires. A human of common blood. Uses Magical Runes for protection.

The Gaggle
"The only blood of importance, is the spilled blood of our enemies."

Goose - Knight Commander. A heavy weapons specialist. An OrcMan of Noble Blood.

Swan - A top tier knight. A Light Mage of common blood. A human. Uses a magical book of poetry to manipulate reality.

Parrot - A mid-tier knight. A berserker of common blood. An OrcElf of common blood.

Albatross - A mid-tier Knight. An Anti-Magic Icicle Berserker of common blood.

The Party
"Flying true."

Blue Jay - Knight Commander. A Pilot of Noble Blood. An Elf.

Goshawk - A mid-tier knight. A pilot of common blood. An Elf.

Chickadee - A low tier knight. A pilot of common blood. An Elf.

Earth
"Our Homeworld"

Elite Guards to The Drakon King
"Our lives for our king."

Tempest - An Elf Wind Mage with unimaginable power of Noble Blood. Father to Crow.

Tornado - A Human Weapons specialist with unimaginable power of Noble Blood. He bears a Bloodstone weapon.

Easter - An Elven Creation Mage with unimaginable power of Noble Blood.

The Drakon King - The most proficient Time Mage to ever exist. King of the Earth Empire. Noble Blood of unknown origin, though most likely Earthling.

Charly - Lover of Penguin.

Aesop
"The city under a planetary wasteland"

Kiva - The Bodyguard to the Regent. An Aesopian Mage of common blood. Possesses the ability to summon and control Golems.

Edgor - Attendant to the Regent. A master of Aesopian Cuisine.

Mirai - The Regent of Aesop. A Mage of Noble Blood. Possesses the ability to see the future.

Ali
"A frozen hearth"

Icicle - This is the name given to all inhabitants of Ali. They do not take names themselves.

Icicle Prime - One of three Icicles that has the ability to speak.

Lord Berg - The ruler of the Icicles. A master of Anti-Magic in his own right.

The Lich - An undead lord. Commander of the Undead.

Beast Knights

"Asleep the Weak. Awaken the Beast."

The Chimera King - A mage of unknown species. Ruler of the Beast Knights.

Silverback - A Knight of unknown species.

Lioness - A Beast Knight of unknown species. A mage of growing power.

Mink - A Beast Knight of unknown species.

Kuma - A Beast Knight of unknown species.

Bonobo - An emissary of The Chimera King

In Memoriam

Emma Vallone

Emma, we love you. We miss you.

I know you're somewhere drinking coffee and petting a Golden Retriever as you help us along this adventure.

A Message from the Author

This book has been seven years of my life. That's three jobs, a wedding, my best friend's weddings, a pandemic, the birth of my child, and a million moments of life, love, stress, and setbacks. I originally set out to call this the acknowledgements page, but really these are my final thoughts on *The Drakon King* before moving on to *The Chimera King* in earnest.

Before I acknowledge anyone else, my wife, Grace, has been my absolute biggest supporter in this process. She's dealt with my rambling about imaginary people every day since we've been together. She's made me go to bed on nights where I've written myself into a corner with no clue how to fix it so that I can "look at it with fresh eyes in the morning." Most importantly, her existence as the other adult in my house has stopped almost everyone else from receiving thousands of phone calls and text messages about Golems and Ice Noughts.

My daughter, Edalyn, is also to thank. Having her is my inspiration to continue pursuing all my dreams, if only to teach her that there are no limits to what she can do.

I am a member of a fantastic family. I have great parents, grandparents, siblings, cousins, aunts, uncles, nieces, nephews, and in-laws. All of whom are supportive, loving, and passionate about a multitude of subjects. You all inspire me daily.

I'm also part of a found family of people that influenced a lot of characters that are in this story and the series. Ally, Lauren, Marijke, Doug, Desmond, Andy, Patterson, Steve, Christian, Carolyn, and Paige; you all are my best friends and I'm positive that there are many more adventures to be had.

I especially want to note Ally Ruiz Talcott, my most consistent editor and most trusted friend, who has literally been there from my first draft of my first college creative writing piece to the last sentence of this novel and has read everything in between. Without you, I certainly wouldn't be the writer I am today, and I definitely wouldn't be the person either. Even if you did so by force at times. If you ever find yourself with a friend like Ally, you are lucky.

This project would also have been harder to complete without Andy Swanson and Simone Brock as sounding boards throughout the entire process. Andy has given me a ton of nerdy ideas over the years and I'm just glad to have him here. Simone actually gave me the original idea when she told me I should "write something about golems."

I want to thank you the reader. If reading this story helps you escape the craziness of this world for a bit of time, then I've done my job as a writer.

I lastly want to acknowledge the idea that anybody can accomplish their goals regardless of skin color or circumstances. Finding Black authors meant the world to me before I was a writer, and still does to this day. If I can give someone hope, then I've succeeded as a person.

www.ingramcontent.com/pod-product-compliance
Lightning Source LLC
Chambersburg PA
CBHW031317170626
46807CB00002B/452